INFILTRATION

A Novel
By
Lee W. Dodson

Edited by Nicole Petrone

Foreword

I first heard of Lee Dodson and *Infiltration* a few years ago, while working at a security magazine. As the managing editor of that publication, most of what crossed my desk were product descriptions and articles about often very high-tech equipment designed, among other things, to increase personal and corporate surveillance, prevent homeland terrorism in its various guises, and tighten border security.

No novels were crossing my desk.

But then there was Lee's book, and just from reading its synopsis, I could tell it would resonate with the magazine's audience.

Intrigued, I took the book home that night and, in truth, after reading the first page I don't remember putting it down. The piece I wrote about the book the next day for that month's issue was the first and still only fiction review ever to appear in that magazine's pages.

Without presenting spoilers, the gist of the piece was that while *Infiltration* is indeed a novel, the particulars of the plot in the violent, bloody, and often tense book you're now holding (or scrolling) are, unfortunately, all too plausible.

Also in the review, I described the book's hero, a 67-year-old Arizona rancher named Rand, as a cross between Tommy Lee Jones in "No Country For Old Men" and Sly Stallone in "Rambo." In retrospect, I could and maybe should have written that another vital part of the Rand mix is Lee himself. If you've read other of his works or perhaps caught him as a guest on talk radio—or, even better, had the opportunity to talk to the man one on one—you'll recognize from whence Rand's resourcefulness, perseverance, compassion, and patriotism come.

I remember calling Lee the day after my one-sitting reading of his book. He was gracious and patient with my questions. I asked him about his writing. He told me he was mainly interested in writing stories that would entertain someone for a few hours and afterward be thrown away—the kind of tales that might be read on a long flight but then left behind for someone else upon landing, is I think how he put it.

I was impressed with the humility and altruism of that answer, but now that it's been almost three years since he told me that, I can attest that even if you are such a reader—the kind who would toss or "gift" this book when you're done—there are certain vivid parts of it that you'll keep with you long after the fact. Some parts of it might well even infiltrate your sleep.

But, meanwhile, prepare to be entertained.

Ronnie Rittenberry

Chapter One

Old Dogs, Bad Boys, and Whatever is Handy

They came in sometime after two on a moonless night. He was not as prepared as he should have been. He was prepared all right, just not as prepared as he should have been. One never is.

Rand had generally ignored the signs, the precursors. Old habits had died the death of atrophy, or at least he told himself they did; but they came back, re-emerged on the first, unmistakable sound of a silenced gunshot, then another at the far end of the long, sprawling ranch house.

The first shot had roused him from his usual late night snooze on the leather couch in front of the big screen in the den. He saw the low flash of the second shot in the hallway that ran the length of the west side of the house. Any light in the darkened house would naturally play the full eighty feet along the corridor. Rand rolled off the couch as the next two pops sounded and crawled toward the gun cabinet. His hand brushed ever so slightly against the slippered foot of the old woman who still snored softly in the recliner-- or she was praying, one never knew which.

He glanced up to see her still asleep, mouth open. Good. Rand continued crabbing across the ten feet to the cabinet, holding low so as not to cast any telltale shadow in case there were more intruders watching. Outside, there were voices. Not good.

Though he couldn't hear them moving towards him yet, Rand speculated that there were at least two inside the house. Two more quick shots sounded by the time he'd opened the drawer that held the handguns and ammo. Rand got to his knees, groped into the felt lined box, and found the Sig, wrapped in an oiled cloth. He jammed four magazines into his left pocket and laid the pistol on the rug between himself and the portal that opened on the hallway. He found his assault knife and slipped it into his belt slanted right, just above his rear end.

The rancher fell back to the floor, picked up the Sig, and crawled toward the hallway portal as quietly as he could. It was easy, even for an old man. He swore under his breath that he had kicked off his boots earlier. He dared not make a sound, which might rouse the old woman and tip off the intruders. If she would just stay asleep for two more minutes…

The sound of soft footfalls came from the hallway, the sounds that rubber soles made when moving along clay tiles. Next, Rand heard a fork hit the tile, and he knew they were at the kitchen, maybe ten feet from the front door. They were fifteen seconds away, twenty if they were scanning for anyone else. Outside, sounds of bodies moving around floated up the barren slope toward the house.

Rand figured at least ten, maybe more. Not good. He came to his knees near the wall at the portal. He let his breath out slowly and used the few seconds to think out the situation.

The rancher was certain that his wife, Carol, and his son, Chuck, were already dead. Four shots at close range on sleeping people were hard to miss, and he and the old woman would join them in short order if he weren't smart. He "safetied" the Sig, jammed it into his belt, and withdrew the assault knife from his back. This would be close-- if it worked at all.

Rand knew from experience that the first guy would come in low with the second guy crouched above him. He heard the hinges on the door to the old woman's room creak. No pops. He realized these guys had to have night vision scopes. He strained to listen and heard the faint whine of older gear. He had five seconds.

Rand crouched, knife at the ready.

As he had guessed, the front man did come in low. Not difficult because the lead guy was short. When he cleared the portal, the rancher grabbed his shirt, pulled him closer, and drove the assault knife into the side of his throat. Blood went everywhere. Rand pivoted the crumpling body around, and blood shot toward the second man, splattering his night vision equipment, and rendering him blind. The rancher yanked the knife free.

While the first man writhed on the floor, the second fired a burst of wild shots. Rand got a hand on the weapon and directed the hot barrel upward as the second man fired another burst. Again, Rand drove the knife for the second man's throat, but the knife found no purchase. The man went down, making little gurgling noises. The rancher realized that both intruders wore body armor, which was why the sideways attack worked, and the frontal approach didn't.

Rand had put enough force into his knife that he had broken the guy's windpipe. The gurgling sound was a familiar, if old, sign. The man was still dangerous, so Rand lifted the throat covering and finished him off. Again, a lot of blood. The rancher's socks were soaked, making him slip on the hall floor when he went to the nearest window to check the situation in front of the house. He scanned the dark interior to see if anybody else was inside.

Nobody.

Good.

He'd done the job, but his first glance outside scared him. Not that he wasn't scared enough already. In the distance, maybe two hundred yards west, where the road from the highway met the perimeter fence, lights from a vehicle flicked on and moved across the desert sand toward the parking area in front of the ranch house. The light swept the dusty landscape across the front of the house, and Rand ducked to the side of the window, but not before he saw five or six men in battle gear standing between his pickup and Carol's Caddy. Brick, his Rhodesian lay on the flagstone walk halfway between the low stone fence and the veranda that ran parallel outside to the long hallway inside. The dog did not move. Rand had wondered why the dog had sent up no alarm. Now, he knew why.

The rancher further noted three other armed men walking casually toward the northeast corner of the house in the direction of the stable. Not good. Somewhere in the back of his mind he heard Brandon deWilde pleading "There's too many, Shane. Too many." Yeah, right.

Going out the front door was out of the question. Rand's best option, short of shooting his way out, up to now, was to get to the stable, get on a fast horse and head north into the flats. Risky, but Bianca, the quarter-horse mare was big, sure-footed, pretty fast, could carry double, and, most of all, co-operative. She'd do it…if he could get to her. Her one trick of laying down on command would serve well in the scrubby desert.

South was not going to happen. The highway was two miles to the south. All these guys would have to do is jump in the vehicles and cut them off in minutes. East was bad, too. The ranch house backed up to a steep hill, steeper as it proceeded south, shallower as it trailed north. It was high, and the slopes were totally exposed, even on a dark night, and it was pretty steep. Bianca was good on everything but hills.

Rand had a minute, perhaps two to get his plan together. He felt the anger creep up into his neck, but he stanched it, not willing to give satisfaction to the men who were on his property. He assumed this was a stealth operation, which could evolve into a full-blown assault if he kept the men out front unaware of his presence.

The rancher caught a glimpse of movement off to his right. The old woman, oblivious to any of the night's activities, was out of the recliner, groping around for her walker to the right of the chair. He crossed the den to her side and hugged her to him.

"Be real quiet and don't move. I need you to sit down for a minute," he whispered into her left ear, the good one. She sat, sensing the urgent tone. Her mouth moved, she prayed silently as she always did. "Preserve my life, O Lord. And that of my preserver." Praying was as much a habit for her as breathing.

Rand returned to the bodies of the men he'd just killed and stripped them of the body armor and one of the silenced rifles. He crossed back to the front of the couch and stepped into his boots, making the move simultaneously while donning the body armor.

He was faster than he expected. It had been years since he'd put the heavies on. Rand pulled the old woman out of her seat and draped the remaining body armor around her shoulders, moving her toward the large windows that opened on the low-walled patio situated between the house and the service road that bordered the stable. The road split left to go north to the barn and right to the utilities behind the house.

In the distance, a staccato report came from the direction of his closest neighbors, Jug and Emma. The rancher clenched his teeth at the thought that these two eighty year olds were suffering the fate his wife and son and Brick had suffered.

"Estufo?" (Done?) Came a shout from the front of the house. "Cinco…eran cinco," (Five, there were five.) Rand called back. The caller laughed. The laugh sounded vaguely familiar, but he couldn't place it. "Fuera te," (Get out of there.) Luc checked the bodies one more time.

He decided that these guys had been trained, very little, but trained nonetheless. They had night vision, camo, all old stuff, but camo was camo. He knew that the Mexicans bought good stuff. These guys were decidedly not military. He couldn't see if they were Latin, but the fact that the leader had called out in Spanish was a pretty good indication.

The trick now would be getting out. Alone, he stood a fifty-fifty chance depending on how many were out there. The odds dropped big time if there were more. Worse, if they were trained.

Rand picked up the old woman and lifted her out the window to the patio. He saw three men carrying flashlights, ambling toward the stable like they were on a Sunday stroll. They had not seen him because their attention rested solely on the stable. To his left, the rancher spotted four heavyset men between his truck and Carol's Caddy. He heard smashing glass and saw the men light flares and toss them inside the vehicles.

This was the good news. The glare from the fuzees would blind them to him, if only for a moment. It might be enough. The old woman stood very still, muttering something unintelligible, not that she ever made sense.

"Don't go anywhere," he rasped.

"I won't. Having done all, stand," she replied calmly.

Rand vaulted back into the den, picked up one of his assailant's rifles, and strode toward the front door, hoping to catch the fire starters unaware. The door was wide open, and when he approached he saw the lights of another car or truck coming down the dirt road toward the house. Maybe it was help; maybe it wasn't. He guessed it was more bad news because he did not see emergency lights.

When he got to the door, Rand peeked around the jamb to spot his targets. They had backed away from the burning vehicles and were looking toward the approaching SUV, coolly motioning it in. He was due for a little luck, and he found it.

These guys were so sure of themselves that they had taken off their helmets and were lighting cigars all around. The SUV was still a good hundred yards away, the flames from the fires kept him hidden. Rand raised the assault rifle and fired four shots in quick succession, hitting the nearest guy first and working his way forward. They went down without a sound. He was grateful they were close enough to take a good hit with the silencer still on the weapon.

The rancher checked the magazine. It was almost full. He fired off a volley of six in the direction of the SUV, walking the shots up till he was confident he had scored on the driver's side windshield.

The SUV stopped immediately, the doors flew open, and he saw bodies spill out both sides to take cover. Good. Rand sprinted back toward the den, slipping on the bloody tile, almost falling, and then he jumped out the patio window. The old woman was still standing a few feet away. "Fire," she said in a matter of fact tone, pointing toward the stable. Somewhere behind him, gunfire erupted, and he heard slugs hit the front of the house and glass smashing.

The three men who were torching the stable were so intent on their work that they paid no attention to the gunfire because the horses in the stable ran for the corral rails in an effort to escape the fire. The men shot Bianca, her colt, and the thoroughbred in a very businesslike fashion, Rand thought, but the big draft horse bucked and reared with such violence that the shots they fired missed. The stud, Gunpowder, lay on the ground, quivering his last.

The three stood for a moment, admiring their success before making an attempt to get the draft horse. Their backs were still toward the rancher, but they still wore their body armor, making a clean shot impossible. Rand had to be careful; one miss was a death sentence. He sat on the low patio wall and swung his legs over as quietly as he could. Then he crouched low and moved deliberately toward them, his eyes roving back and forth over the trio.

The smallest man of the three hurried closer to the corral rails to get a better angle on Bianca's foal and the big draft horse. The foal dropped after a shot to the chest, and the shooter shielded his face from the heat, closed in, and put the foal out with another shot to its head. The other two made remarks about him needing practice, and the little man shifted his stance to draw a bead on the draft.

Rand had closed to within twenty-five yards of the two closest; the little guy was about thirty-five yards directly in front of him. The noise and glare of the flaming stable was enough to keep their attention, and enough to keep them from hearing the rancher who closed in, deciding his shots.

The draft was all that was left, and the rancher needed a mount-- and he needed headshots. He sprinted toward the two closest. As he came abreast of the two nearest, he steadied and fired once at the little man. It was a perfect send. The little man collapsed straight down, shocking the two left.

By now, Rand was between the two remaining men. He lunged for the ground, firing once at the man on his left. The round struck the man's body armor at the chest bone, and his target stumbled backward, trying to recover. The rancher fired twice more and heard the man scream.

Rand rolled towards his right, hoping the last man was surprised enough to pause not wanting to hit his compatriot. The assailant came at him firing as he approached. It was serious, but not lethal. The rancher's stolen body armor did its job. He took six rounds and felt every one of them. Two more shots went wild as he came to his knees.

Rand fired once and saw the night vision fly off the man's head. The man took two steps back and fell flat on his side. The rancher got to his feet and glanced over his shoulder to discover that the assailant to his left was not dead, but was trying to get to his feet. When the man's helmet fell off, the rancher shot him through the top of his head.

There was no time to waste. Rand could see the war party carefully making their way toward the front of the house. He noticed they used the right tactics.

Some lay down covering fire, while others advanced. They were trained all right. As he made for the corral gate and for the draft, he realized that, in their zeal to take the front of the house, these idiots had apparently forgotten to send out flankers. So far, his luck held.

The rancher approached the gate where the big, black draft horse pranced in place, waiting to be let out and away from the fire. When the horse recognized Rand, he settled down, knowing that the rancher would not hurt him. Beamer was a big horse, seventeen and some; he pawed at the ground and grunted impatiently. "Damn good horse," was all he said, "Easy," and he reached through the gate to grab a handful of mane.

Beyond this little corral was another larger round pen where the brood mares waited to foal. Rand pulled Beamer along to the next gate and released his four best mares and a little roan filly. They were out and galloping away in an instant. Beamer wanted to go, too, but as long as Rand held his mane, the draft would not move.

The rancher was suddenly very tired. There was no way he was going to be able to mount the draft from the ground, so he pulled the big horse closer to the corral rails, which, of course, was closer to the burning stable. Beamer was having none of it, but Rand insisted, and got his way. He climbed up two levels, and as he did, the rancher heard the characteristic whistles of two rounds coming by, close enough to make him duck.

"I'll be damned," he thought out loud. "They were smart enough to send out flankers." With that he spotted two muzzle flashes a good fifty yards north of his position and heard the whistling cracks. Rand had no choice. He could not return fire unless he wanted to lose the horse. Mane in one hand, rifle in the other, he leapt from the fence onto the draft's back, and the horse lumbered forward toward the house.

Parthian shots are a waste of ammo. They run wild and only serve to make the enemy take cover until they realize backward shots are what they are. Basically, they were nothing but expensive prices on time. Rand decided, as the slugs sailed past him, one hitting the back of his flak jacket, he'd chance it just this once. He lay low on Beamer's back and fired a burst full auto at where he'd last seen the flashes.

The burst did what it always did. It bought a few seconds…no more, but it was enough time to urge Beamer toward the patio wall.

Beamer was not fast, but he was strong, and he was determined. He knew where the rancher wanted him to go, and he went toward the patio.

Rand saw the war party advancing on the front of the house. To avoid being seen as a rider, he slung over to Beamer's left side Comanche style. With his head under the horse's neck, he saw two men making their way for the space between the patio and stable. They paid little attention to the horse. They focused on the house.

Beamer approached the patio wall like he'd done so many times in the past. The horse was so people-friendly that he would wait for Carol to call him, and he'd open his own gate to come get a treat from her hand at the patio wall. He had not been calm enough to open his own gate during the fire, but with the fire yards behind him, the draft came to his exact spot to wait for Carol. He was a rescue horse in lieu of a new BMW, thus the name.

The two men who rounded the corner of the house were still thirty yards west, and with all the confusion of the burning stable, the bodies of their compatriots near the stable, the bodies of the men who'd torched the truck and Caddy, they were taking no risk. Rand figured they were forty or fifty yards away, and he still had to get into the patio, pick up the old woman, get her onto the horse, and get away, so he laid down a few shots to distract them.

It worked. They ran toward the cover of the corner of the house, firing wildly as they took cover. Meanwhile Rand was luckier than he thought he would be. By some miracle, when the draft's head reached over the wall for his treat, the old woman was standing on the wall like a schoolgirl waiting for a carpool ride.

More rounds came in from the flankers who had recovered from the backward shots off the horse. The slugs thudded into the patio wall, the wall of the house, and finally struck one of Carol's antique hurricane lamps, sending kerosene splashing onto the chaise below it. From Beamer's back, Rand scooped the old woman off the wall and plunked her onto the horse's shoulders sidesaddle style. In less than five seconds, the rancher kicked flank to move Beamer away from the wall.

The rancher had nowhere to go. The flankers were moving in from the north fifty yards or so from the burning stable, and he couldn't see them. The war party had the front of the house aswarm with who knows how many. So his first plan was out.

On the bright side, if there was one, Beamer was one powerful son of a bitch, and he could take the hill behind the house without breaking a sweat…Rand hoped. Since it was their only chance, he wheeled the draft left and kicked him into action. Another round came by and hit the patio lamp, sending sparks onto the kerosene soaked chaise and touching off a fire.

Rand reached into the pocket of the flak jacket and found one magazine. He tossed it, hoping it would land on the chaise and cook off the rounds as a diversion. The magazine found its mark, but nothing happened. He slung the rifle around in front of the old woman and fired a burst in the direction of the flankers. He kicked the horse's flanks and clucked, and Beamer lunged forward from a standstill to a lope in three steps.

The old woman murmured, "I will lift up my eyes to hills whence comest my help. My help comes from the Lord."

"He better get here soon," the rancher commented.

The flankers continued fire, but the rounds were shy for a few seconds, enough time for the mounted party to get past the perimeter of light from the stable. The rancher knew that the night vision would be pretty useless with all the light from the stable fire and, now, from the fire in the patio. Precious seconds.

They ascended the hill, Beamer coming to what could be called a gallop. On any other horse, it would be called a lope. Behind them, shouts and orders poured from the front of the house. Somebody was pretty ticked off, Rand mused. Whether he said it out loud or not, he would not remember, but old woman muttered, "Sounds pretty mad to me."

The two who had taken cover at the corner of the house, came around to the road between the stable and the house, and began to lay down fire, walking it up the hill toward Rand and the old woman. He turned and saw the sand spurt up where the slugs hit and the muzzle flashes from the silhouetted figures kneeling on the road. He planted the butt of the rifle under his arm and pulled the trigger. Nada. He felt in the pockets of the flak jacket for another magazine. Nada, again. He tossed the weapon away, hearing it land and slide down the hillside.

Beamer turned slightly left, not wanting to climb straight up the hill, and this gave the rancher a chance to see the situation fifty yards below at the base of the hill. The fires revealed a squad of men taking firing positions, kneeling and prone. Rand saw the flankers come in and set up shop twenty yards uphill and away from the stable. He wished for a rifle. Then, he saw something really scary: a tall man with a long case walking casually toward the group.

Rand knew what this was. Beamer turned right and continued his ascent crosswise of the hill. The rancher thought for a second. The tall guy was a sniper, and from his deliberate pace, this was a guy who knew his business. The case appeared to be an HK .50, capable of tearing anything it hit apart.

The rancher had to do something. He slowed the horse, making him track sideways along the hillside. "Can you straddle?" he asked the old woman. "'Bout damn time," she muttered. "Never went for girlie ridin'." She slid her right leg over Beamer's shoulders. "'Lot better." The rancher pulled the Sig from his belt and let Beamer trail along until they were directly behind the now burning house. He knew that when he took his shot, it would draw fire to his present position. As it was, the war party was just shooting in the dark at the last place they'd seen him.

Rand stopped Beamer and turned him north. This would be high risk. "Hang on to his mane," he whispered. "Gonna teach me to suck eggs next, El Paso?" she rasped back. "Ready when you are. I will not fear the arrows that fly by day."

"How 'bout the bullets that fly by night?"

Rand fired two quick shots and heard them clank when they struck their target. He kicked Beamer hard and was able to get one more "insurance" shot off before Beamer came to a real gallop. Making a horse move fast, especially a draft horse, on a steep slope, running sideways to the hill was about as dangerous as anything on horseback.

The last shot hit its mark better than the other two. The space between the house and stable erupted with continuing gunfire, but nothing close to them. The war party was ranging on the position from where Rand had fired. He slowed Beamer to a walk to conserve his energy, and then the rancher strained to hear if he had been successful with the tactic.

Below, the tall man had assembled his weapon and took his position. Rand could tell from this distance that the guy was equipped with infrared sighting. The rancher, the old woman, and the horse were sitting ducks. There was no cover on the hillside, not even a big rock. There was just sand, gravel, and a few scrub brushes. He knew they would not clear the top in time.

"What's that sound" the woman whispered. The rancher couldn't hear it. "That whistle."
Rand suddenly urged the horse forward. "We gotta go," he said, and he attempted a glimpse of the war party as they moved. He wanted to find the wildlife path that followed from the house to the top of the hill. The going was easier, not as many rocks or as much sand.

The rancher saw below what he was looking for: little ripples of air like a distant mirage on the highway, and not a moment too soon. The tall man had found them in his sights and followed them, seemingly amusing himself with the prospect of an easy kill shot. After all, they were less than halfway to the crest. He had plenty of time. A pro could fire as many as ten shots in a few minutes. It would take that long to clear the top.

Rand wondered if this guy was trying to decide whom to kill first. The rancher knew long range guys like that, ones who toyed with their targets in their heads. He never had any respect for guys like that, but he was glad this guy was like that.

The rancher had not fired the Sig at the war party. He had deliberately fired at the LPG tank at the back of the house. He had hoped that the first shot would penetrate the steel tank's side, low enough to be under the fuel level. The second shot he wanted to enter high enough to be above the fuel level. LPG, being heavier than air, would leak out and follow the terrain. In this case, he hoped it would trail down to the area between the house and the stable.

The little dancing airwaves told him he was right, but he was not sure it would be in time. Rand looked back toward the road and caught glimpse of two more sets of headlights coming toward the ranch house. That can't be good, he thought to himself. The old woman saw the lights, too. "More. My enemy hems me in at all sides," was all she said.

A little red dot of light that appeared on the side of Beamer's head alarmed him. The war party wouldn't be able to see it, but the sniper could.

The dot steadied behind Beamer's ear. Rand knew what it meant. He steadied the draft for just a moment, a second really…waited, and when the red dot made a tiny jump, the rancher reined the horse right, fast and hard, and hoped he made his move in time.

In less than a second, a fifty came by his left year. Beamer did his usual spin all the way around like a reining horse, slipped sideways a few feet, came to a full stop, facing the same way as he'd started. Rand reined right once more, taking pressure off as the draft faced uphill. Rand kicked flank hard, and the horse, already frightened by the sound of the slug coming by, needed no further encouragement. He made a gigantic bound forward, not caring whether they were on a trail or not. The draft didn't like where he was and wanted to be somewhere else.

The war party had seen where the sniper fired, and they cut loose with volleys that ceased only when they were reloading. It was a big mistake. By the time they had snapped off thirty full autos, tracing the draft's path, the LPG had reached them and the flames of the house and the stable touched off the petroleum and sent a shock wave up the hill.

Rand didn't have time to look back, but he was sure it wasn't pretty. He urged the horse forward, and Beamer was only too happy to comply. The tactic was successful. The gunfire stopped, but the rancher knew the lull was temporary. There were another sixty or seventy yards to the rounded rim of the hill to make. Only then would they reach cover.

Beamer coughed hard, laboring under the load and the climb, but the old boy was gallant. He would have done anything for Carol. He seemed to realize she'd rescued him from being put down a few years ago. Now, his loyalty transferred to either Rand or the old woman. Whatever, he gave the climb everything he had and then some. Horses will do that.

The climb and the momentary quiet made him think back. Carol and Chuck were gone. The first four shots made sure of that. The ranch was gone. All he had left was Beamer and the old woman, and he was none too sure how long they could last. A beat up old draft horse and an eighty-year old Alzheimer's patient, not good odds for survival, but then again, neither were his.

Rand, at sixty-seven, had seen better days. Drafted out of a failing college career, straight into Nam where he'd done three tours, battlefield commissioned to captain because everybody else was dead, the rancher went all the way to instructor in special ops till he slugged a bird colonel at Ft. Lewis, and retired on a sergeant's pay rating to the ranch to raise horses. The hard work was what kept him alive, or so Carol said.

The ranch was her idea. He wanted nothing more than to sit in an air-conditioned house near a garage and drink beer all day, but she wasn't having it. She was going to have horses, and like every second wife, she generally got her way.

The old woman was her idea, too. Although she was Rand's aunt, Carol insisted that Amy stay with them after she was diagnosed. The disease progressed slowly with the drugs, so aside from being a little slow on her feet and having odd lapses of memory, the old woman was a decent presence in the house. For some reason, Amy got along with Chuck who had crashed into puberty in one day. The two "got" each other.

Amy was beautiful once upon a time. She still had grace and was as vain as the witch in the mirror in Snow White. Now, she was thin and tough as high plains barbed wire. Carol said Amy was what Scarlett O'Hara would have been in later years. Chuck said she was just crazy enough to be interesting. Rand's wife and son did most of the talking.

Life on the ranch had calmed Rand, or maybe it was Carol, or Chuck, or the old woman, or all of them. The silver haired six-footer stood in stark contrast to the little blond woman. He was rangy rawhide and she was zaftig silk. The only physical trait they shared was the blue of their eyes, like their son's.

Gone.

The going was easier for the moment as the fire below lit up the hillside. Beamer was better when he could see. He had slowed a bit, but they were making good time. In a few minutes, horse and riders cleared the crest of the hill. Rand turned the horse in time to see the blue flame run from the road between house and stable back to the tank. He saw the intruders either burning on the ground or scrambling to dowse their burning clothing. The sniper's body was charred, hands still on the fifty calibers.

The still fiery stable was flattened by the dint of the explosion, but the house still stood, but not for long. The trailing blue flame reached the LPG tank, and sent it rocketing skyward like an out of control, wounded Agena, a plume of flame spurting out a rupture in its side. When it reached fifty feet, well below Rand's vantage point, the tank heeled over like a giant pinwheel, making an arc over the house, and landing near the SUV at the edge of his cleared land. When it hit the ground, the weakened cylinder burst and exploded, setting ablaze the SUV.

The force of the second explosion took the tiled roof off the ranch house and sent it backward into the hillside and touching off the interior of the house. Three of the still standing intruders were engulfed in the fireball, the remaining were knocked off their feet, two falling into the burning collapsed stable.

The far headlights had not moved since the gas caught. Rand saw them reverse, stop, then wink out. He could barely see the interior lights come on. It meant somebody was leaving the vehicles.

The night was remarkably still. Smoke rose straight up. In the distance, a spread of light flickered, meaning that, indeed, Jug and Emma's place was on fire. Rand spent no time wondering why. He shook his head. They were nice people.

"It's bad, isn't it," Amy asked softly.

"Yeah. Bad," was all he wanted to answer as he dismounted and helped her off the horse. Amy wrapped her arms around his right shoulder and allowed him to gently hoist her down, pausing to let her feet find the ground before he let her go.

"Oughta leave me here. The Lord will see to me," Amy had grit all right.

"Nope. Can't. He hired me for that job."

"Carol and the boy?" She already knew the answer, but she asked it anyway.

"Don't think they had a chance," he replied and led the draft away from the sight lines of the hilltop.

Rand heard the motors on the SUVs start, heard them plow over the scrub that lined the roadway, moving in the direction of the burning ranch house.

Because sound carries so well in the desert, especially when the air is still, the rancher heard clearly the angry shouting when the vehicles came to a stop. He stopped the horse with a word and helped the old woman to a place where she and the animal could stand without being discovered. Then he crept back to the edge of the hill to get a look at the situation.

"You good?" he asked.

"Good," she replied.

"Stay right here by Beamer, okay?"

When she answered "Okay," Rand turned toward the rim for a look. He ran his hands over his chest and as much as he could reach of his back, then down his legs to see if he'd taken any slugs. He was bruised from the rounds hitting the flak jacket.

He was sore, and the adrenaline was spent. Rand was tired. What was it, three o'clock? Had to be. Felt longer, but firefights have their own clocks. He ran his hands over the lathered draft, paying particular attention to Beamer's rump, and he found it. The horse had been hit high on the right side of his hindquarters. It was hard to tell how bad in the darkness and with the lathering, but he did find a small hole, which made Beamer start when Rand touched it.

The rancher gingerly ran his fingers forward and felt a lump an inch away where the slug had stopped. Fortunately, the lead had not pierced muscle. It lay right beneath the hide. Uncomfortable, but not life threatening. He ejected a cartridge, pulled the lead out. And dabbed the gunpowder in the entry point.

"Is he hurt bad?" Amy rasped. Rand took her hand and put it on the opening. She pulled away, and he thought she was repulsed by the blood, but to the contrary, the old woman bent down and ripped a piece of her robe from the bottom, wadded it up and applied it to the wound.

"I need to go look. You be okay?"

"Go. The Lord is my shepherd."

He made himself get on all fours to pick his way across the twenty or thirty yards to the edge of what he called a hill. It was actually a mesa, so long standing that its edges had fallen off in so many places that it had less definition than a true mesa.

When the rancher met the edge, he could hear every heated word of the last arriving group while they surveyed the damage.

The house was fully engulfed in flame. Big men with bull-pup weapons skirted the perimeter of the fires, stooping to throw sand on the burning bodies of the first raiding party. Screams and groans emanated from the scattered who still lived, and one, who seemed to be in command, paced quickly back and forth, shouting and mixing his cursing in English and in Spanish into a cell phone.

The good news was that no one had given chase--
yet. They were busy collecting what they could of the
dead and wounded. Rand saw the bodies of the men
who had torched his vehicles sticking out from under
the pickup, counted nine more between the house and
stable, including the sniper. A few of those caught in
the secondary explosion lay near the front gate, one
of them moving, trying to crawl away.

The two SUVs sat, doors open, idling, and another
came racing down the approach road, veered
suddenly to miss the vehicle on fire, bounced over
the berm, and crashed through Rand's perimeter
fence. It drove directly for the big man, slammed on
the brakes, and skidded to a stop.

Another large, well-dressed man exited the driver's
side and strode to the one on the cell phone. The man
from the SUV was clearly in charge. He bore in on
the other and got in his face. Rand could not hear the
conversation, but judging from body language, it was
intensely unpleasant. The talk lasted a minute or so,
then the well-dressed man pulled a Bushmaster from
under his jacket, walked toward the wounded men,
and casually shot each one in the head.

The others in the second party froze until the well-
dressed man barked an order, telling the party to
collect the bodies. Rand decided to call this guy
Guapo, the other Cujo. Big fat guys. Cujo went to
one of the SUVs and produced a high intensity light
while the crew retrieved body bags from the back. It
helped giving them names.

Pretty organized, Rand thought to himself. What the hell is this all about? But the question dead stopped in his head when Cujo began to play the light beam along the hillside where Beamer had carried him. The light stopped here and there, and there was some discussion between the two men.

The rancher heard the words "Siga lo," and knew instantly what it meant. They were going to follow him. He remained motionless. It was all he could do to keep himself still.
"Traeme la cabeza," (Bring me his head.)

He was tired, bone tired, and he wanted to run, but Rand thought that he didn't know enough, so he lay where he was, putting on his "recon" eyes to see if these guys were any good, see if they had tactics, see what they were going to do. Most of all, he wanted to know how they would follow him.

They knew how to use flankers. The stable assault proved that. The rancher strained to hear. Behind him, Beamer snorted, and Amy spoke soothing words. Below the recovery party finished their work, but they dared not enter the house or the stable area. The clean up was quick, professional, and they assembled around the leader, Guapo.

The war party knew what they were doing. Of twelve grunts, six grouped at the base of the hill directly below him. Three split off to his left, maybe thirty yards, and the other three split left, at an equal distance. Cujo joined the main party.

The three to Rand's left would have the toughest climb. The hill rose steeply and could only be scaled on all fours. They would take the most time, and they were the most exposed. If he had a rifle, he would make a stand here.

The center party had to be on guard for counter attack, so they would leap frog their way up. Time consuming. Their flankers would need time to assist in case Rand decided to do a shoot and run. He was certain they had no clue as to his weapons situation. On the other side, to his right, the hill rose more gradually. They would catch the ridge then have to turn right to hit the rim, or they would stay in the flats to circle around to cut him off.

The rancher counted the number. Twelve men made up the assault party. Three on his left, the southern flankers, looked pretty strong. All about the same size and weight. Three on his right, were shorter, one guy really too fat to be any kind of a threat, but you never knew.

The six in the center appeared to follow a little guy who walked like a bantam rooster. He turned his back on Cujo with disdain and spoke to his crew, motioning toward the hill, and then he spoke orders to the flankers who fanned out to their respective starting points. Rand decided to call the little guy Primero.

Primero knew his business, one of those de facto leaders who made his bones by being the toughest, the meanest, and the nastiest. And it was probable; he was all kinds of bad guy, into drugs, or whatever, a killer.

The rancher wondered if Cujo would join them, but he no longer had time to consider the question. The assault party would set off in minutes, and distance between him and them was a precious commodity.

Chapter Two

Hide When You Can, Fight When You Have To

In the old days, Rand would have done a hit and run with the pistol, but, once again, he heard the little boy in Shane say, "There's too many." Plus there was the added presence of Amy. She would offer to stay behind, as before, but this was a no go for him.

Rand had two hundred yards on them, hard, steep, and exposed yards. He, on the other hand, had flats for three miles until the path came to a deep arroyo. Beamer could do the distance in a trot and make the arroyo before the war party met up on the rim of the mesa. The rancher formulated a plan as he stood and walked back to the horse and old woman.

First things first, he mused as he lifted Amy onto Beamer's back. Rand decided he was too tired to try to mount the big horse, so he led him with his hand under the horse's jaw. Beamer would get the idea and follow on in a few minutes, or until he figured out where the rancher was going.

Atop the draft Amy still prayed. "As the deer pants for water, so my soul pants for Thee." It was her pattern, scriptural metaphor. Carol figured it out first and knew the difference between the old woman's prayers and spoken needs.

Rand was parched, and it was sure that Beamer needed water, too. The arroyo normally had standing water in it this time of year, the end of the "monsoon" season. There could be more rain coming up from Baja. It had rained two days ago, so chances for water in the arroyo were good.

He, of course, opted for the arroyo because it was good cover and because he could follow it north to the flats without being seen. He'd scrounged up many a head of cattle and horses in this gully. They liked it for the shade. It was so deep that the sun stayed on it midday from eleven to two; it was an oven then, but the rest of the time it was more than comfortable.

There was only one problem with the arroyo, and that was that it was apt to cave in at the sides because the soil was loose and during rains boulders would roll down from the mountain whence the arroyo originated. It could be a death trap during a storm, but for now, it held precious water that they needed.

Near the base of the mountain, the walls of the gully had collapsed many times leaving gradual ramps on either side which livestock used easily. Running north and south, the depression grew wider the further north it trailed. When it finally reached the basin, really an ancient seabed, the arroyo forked in four directions.

Rand planned to follow the westernmost gully because it led to a place where he might be able to hunker down and not be seen. This gully was the shallowest of the four, but it was in a direct line for the place he wanted to hide. His exposure would be greater than the other three, but time was short. They could rest there, and he or both of them could go the twenty miles north to a good highway and help.

It was still dark. The east wind kicked up, telling him that sunrise was imminent. He was glad he'd gotten his boots on. The desert was rocky here below the mountain. Rand led them in a scouter's pace. Fifty at a trot, fifty at a walk. He could make about five miles an hour.

The rancher still had no idea about the why of the assault on his ranch or on the others. The drug runners didn't need to do this, nor did the "mojados," or wetbacks. Either of these left him alone: if he steered clear of them, they steered clear of him. But now this didn't make sense.

Beamer suddenly picked up the pace. He smelled water and figured out where they were going. The draft slanted right toward the base of the mountain. He'd been here many times with Carol. He found the sandy ramp and plunged downward almost losing his rider, but Amy was doing well.

Rand tripped and tumbled ass over teakettle and got to his feet in time to hear the horse splashing in water. He followed the sound along the sandy bottom of the crease. It was colder down here, twenty feet below from where they had come.

Amy shivered, trembling as the rancher helped her off the drinking horse. Her robe was soaked from the sweating horse, and she'd lost her slippers somewhere along the way.

It was not as dark, and the chill and the breeze signaled that it would be light soon. Real light. When the sun comes up in the desert, it comes up quicker than you can realize.

They had probably two miles, maybe three, on the assault party. They would be very careful, fearing an ambush and not familiar with the territory. Rand surmised he might have an hour or two on them. Not nearly enough.

"Tired?" he asked.

"Ma-ad," she responded, using the two syllable Texas pronunciation to illustrate her extreme anger like her calling him by his full name when he was a boy.

"Me, too."

"Damn well should be," and she would have continued, but typically, she stopped. No one knew whether she thought the better of saying more or whether she forgot the rest of the sentence. Her drawl was back, meaning she believed she was a schoolgirl in Texarkana again. This was a good sign. In this fugue, she never used a walker, carried herself like a cotillion queen with a wrinkle free face.

Rand was glad to be in the arroyo. On the mesa plain above, wind would have carried sounds down wind into the assault team. Here the sound travelled as far as the arroyo walls, no further.

Beamer snorted, clearing the water from his nostrils, stepping back from the edge to let Rand lay down to drink. Amy knelt beside him and drew water into cupped hands, drinking long drafts. She dipped the hem of her robe in the water and went to Beamer's rump to cleanse the wound. The draft bent his head back to her and bobbed it up and down as if he appreciated the attention.

The rancher didn't want to get up. The sand was still warm from yesterday's sun, but he could not afford the luxury of rest. It would be light in an hour or so, and his pursuers would be able to track the horse and to move faster. He rested for a few minutes.

Amy sized up the rancher in the low light. "Best wash the blood off, El Paso."

The fifty-year-old nickname made him grin.

"Don't do it now, it'll never come out. You're a mess." He stood, shucked off his boots, flak jacket, shirt, and socks. She was right. He was a mess. "Pants, too." She knelt and sloshed the clothing around in the water, scrubbing the fabric against itself. "You wash you. I'll take care of the rest." It was an old skill she'd learned as a missionary's wife on the reservation.

Rand waded into the water. He scrubbed his skin with handfuls of sand silt while the old woman wrung out the clothes and snapped them in the air when Beamer's ears came up. The draft put his head up and looked down the arroyo. He shuffled back and blew his nostrils clear.

This did not go unnoticed by the old woman. She looked in the same direction. "Better check," she said. The tone was one of a woman who'd lived long on the unforgiving ground of the Arizona desert. She tossed Rand the Sig, and he waded carefully north between the west arroyo wall and the water, pistol held high.

The arroyo widened considerably. On his right, across the ponding water, old growth salt cedars hugged the east wall. At one time, they had lined the rim, but they had collapsed into the wash, had taken root and had flourished. The rancher trailed a hundred yards before he heard what had alerted Beamer. It was voices of men speaking Spanish.

That his trackers had arrived so soon was not logical. He wondered if it were illegals crossing north. In any case, Rand didn't want to be seen, so he crossed the water to take cover in the salt cedar growth where he could hear better.

It was clear from their patter that they were confident they had nothing to fear from an old "gabacho" rancher. They laughed as they discussed what they would to do to him. One remarked he would tie the rancher to stakes on an anthill and wait for a day to kill him, but first they would fill his mouth with sand, and would shake it out after they cut off his head. Another big laugh as they walked along the edge of the arroyo looking for a way down to the water.

Rand tracked along the cedar grove, catching a glimpse of them. It was the three north flankers. Their clothing was soaked, indicating they must have run a fair distance, and they had good reason. Guapo had put a bounty of ten thousand American on the rancher, and they talked about what they would do with the money.

Rand knew that thirty yards ahead just after a westward bend, there was another steeper ramp that led from the rim to the bottom of the arroyo. They'd come down there. If he tried to take them on with the Sig, they'd cut him to ribbons. Frontal assault was out of the question. He let the trio follow on to the ramp while he looked for a way up on the east side.

The trees grew close to the wall, so Rand climbed the sturdiest and rolled onto the rim. The water ended within a few yards. There was enough foliage to cover his ascent and transfer to the top, but he noticed the characteristic parallel rifts along the rim. He had to be cautious or he'd collapse the earth and end up sitting on the bottom with nowhere to go.

He caught sight of the men as they cast their eyes south. "Despacio, ellos," one of them said, talking about how slow the others were, a source of comfort to the rancher. Knowing the other parties were behind this one, indicated he had some time.

The rancher lay flat on the ground, hidden by the upper parts of the cedars. He could see the flankers descend the sandy ramp, half sliding, half walking, paying more attention to their footing than to looking for their quarry. Besides, the sun was in their eyes. If Rand had moved, they would have seen him.

He waited till they disappeared into the shadow below him before he moved. He listened for them to divest themselves of packs and gear, and then he crept to the edge to pinpoint them.

The trio, indeed, made their rest stop at the edge of the water near the sturdy salt cedar. After they drank, they sat with their backs resting against the east wall. The rancher peeked over the edge and noted their position relative to the rim. He mentally marked the spot and rolled away from the edge.

From the rim, Rand could snap off three shots easily, but he was unsure where the other parties were. Gunfire would bring nine or ten down on him in an instant. There had to be another way.

Unexpectedly, the rim near the tree where he had climbed up gave out, sending chunks of earth down past the tree, splashing into the water. He heard the men jump to their feet, heard them chamber rounds, and heard them wade to the middle of the grove. The lead man hushed the others and moved quietly to the center of the grove.

Rand sprinted to the eastern ramp and was about a third of the way down when he spotted an outcropping that had been undercut by the storm a few days ago leaving an eight foot deep erosion under ten feet of sandy soil. Rand had missed it because it was completely obscured by the trees.

They were so busy looking that they missed the rancher coming down, and then going back up the ramp. Watching the movement of the trees gave Rand a very good idea where they were.

He noted a good-sized parallel rift immediately above their position and figured it was worth a try. Rand crouched and ran a few yards away from the edge of the arroyo, making sure his shadow did not track across the other sidewall. He drew in his breath, thinking he was glad nobody could see a man in his sixties in tighty whiteys running for the edge of an arroyo.

Six feet from where he wanted to land, the rancher jumped as high as he could and landed three feet from the edge. Nothing happened. He jumped again, hearing the men twenty feet below him stir. Rand was sure they could see his shadow. He decided to jump one more time, and then he'd have to use the Sig.

This time, the ground gave below him, carrying him down, riding the dirt like a surfer rides a wave. It worked better than he expected. The ground behind him collapsed and the entire bluff fell with everything twenty feet either side of him. When the collapse reached bottom, the rancher's legs were buried to the knees, and his trackers were nowhere to be seen. He had fallen ten feet. It had happened so quickly, the men had no time to cry out.

There was nothing left. The trunks of the salt cedars protruded from the newly formed mound. There were sounds of sand running off the side of the arroyo where the collapse had occurred.

The collapse carried all the way to the center of the water. Rand scanned the new hill to see if there was any life. Near the waterline, he detected subsurface movement. He scooped the sand away from his legs and did another recon of the area. The sand near the water turned dark from the water seeping into it.

The sand near the edge moved again. The rancher was surprised to see a small fissure open above the moving earth. It snaked toward the center, broke away, then revealed the sandy image of an arm. The sand shook away and became a real arm. A hand groped as if it were trying to unbury the body to which it was attached.

Rand watched, fascinated by the idea that anyone could have survived. The soil weighed hundreds, if not thousands of pounds. Had this man not been intent on killing him, Rand would have been digging away, but seeing as how this was a very bad guy, he let it go.

Slow death of anyone, even an enemy, bothered the rancher. After a minute, the hand stopped moving. This threat was over.

The sun was high enough to illuminate a quarter of the west wall. His mind returned to the business at hand. The rancher was hungry. Amy probably was, as well, so he set about scavenging what he could.

After checking for a pulse, Rand worked to uncover the body attached to the arm. He pushed sand away until the body was fully exposed. He stripped off the outer clothing, boots, retrieved the ammo from the cargo belt, liberated the AK, and then recovered the body. He trotted back to where the men had left their packs and stuffed food and other essentials, like a first aid kit, into one. He probed the soil one more time and came up with a .40 Browning, too good a weapon for a rag tag outfit. Then he found an overloaded ammo belt, too many for bandits. These guys were loaded for a small revolution. Geez, he thought, this stuff is heavy.

With the clothing over his shoulder, AK in one hand, pack in the other; he worked his way back to the other end of the water to find Amy and Beamer. He had clothing that would serve for Amy. The pants needed to be rinsed out. The crushing had squeezed everything out of the guy.

He was happy to have the AK and the ammo. AKs were sturdy, and the rifle would give him some range if he had to fight again.

In the five minutes it took to return to where he'd left Amy and the draft, the rancher concentrated on his plan.

He needed distance first, and he needed to recapture the time the last sortie had cost him. Second, he needed to get to a defensible position. Rand felt he knew how Vittorio, the last Apache holdout, felt in Dog Canyon. The Seventh Cavalry never caught him, but it was touch and go for months.

Crossing the desert twenty or thirty miles to get to the next highway would leave him exposed unless he traveled at night which was risky. No water that he knew of, no trails but cattle paths.

He considered backtracking Comanche style to the house, but Amy was a total liability if the attackers returned. Besides, the ranch was a great central location. The bad guys would be back.

No, they needed a hideout where she could be safe for a few days while Rand struck out for the highway. He decided on the ruins, a half-day's ride northwest.

It was problematic because the trail to it was not a straight shot, but it did afford some cover due to the scrub and dunes through which the trail wound. Most of the path was rocky, so tracking would be difficult, but like everything this had a downside, in that the rocks were hard on horses' feet. The path was generally a downhill run, but the final half-mile was nothing less than an uphill rock field, open and difficult to navigate for man or horse. ATVs had a rough time on it.

Moving in a northwest direction was "bear smart." Bears make a straight path for a while, then, they track back on a slant. Nobody expects it, but bears. It's one thing that makes them dangerous.

Another good thing was that the ruins were siege defensible. It had natural cisterns of pure rock, and with the rains over the last few days they would be full. Located on a butte that rose maybe ten stories from the rock field, the ruins sat in what was called the Stronghold, a cliff dwelling that was obscured from view, but from an outcropping of solid granite a 270 degree view from northeast to northwest was its crowning point.

He wondered why he hadn't considered the stronghold first thing. Rand thought that he must be getting old. Took a long time to recover.

The rancher assessed his arms situation. He was armed for long range, close quarter, and hand-to-hand. If they could get to the butte undetected, he could take the time to plan longer range, maybe grieve…

His mind stopped mid-thought. Was he in the right place? He waded out of the water onto the sand. Where was the old woman? Where was the horse?

Rand checked the ground beneath his feet. Indeed, Beamer's large hoof prints led directly into the water accompanied by small human prints, but there was no sign of them. He checked again and found no other fresh prints.

"That you, Rand?" the old woman's voice came from the nearest stand of salt cedar twenty yards into the water. The upper limbs parted, and he could see her and the draft standing knee deep behind the clutch of trees. She recognized him and brought the horse out from the hiding place and waded laboriously toward him.

"Didn't seem smart to wait in the open," she murmured. She clutched his clothing to her breast and offered them up. She was soaked. "Fell once," she said when he looked at the robe. He swapped the clothing he'd scavenged for the ones she held, and said
"Put 'em on. We need to go."

She stared at him. "Well," he said impatiently.

"Turn yourself around,"

"Didn't seem to bother you when I stripped off..."

"That was you. This is me."

They stood on opposites sides of Beamer as they dressed.

The rancher had to smile. Amy was a hard case all her life. Lately, she had receded into a state of calm, oddly brought on by the Alzheimer's. Being a missionary's wife was no picnic, but she kept her complaints to herself. They used to say of her that she was too good looking not be anything but impossible. People will put up with a lot from a pretty woman, and so they did with her.

Amy clucked with disgust at the clothing. When she appeared from behind her horse-dressing screen, she had the camo shirt tied at the waist like a teenager, the pants rolled tightly at the ankle of the boots, and a Beretta .380 in her hand.

"Where'd you find that?" Rand asked.

"Pocket." She held it out to him.

"Keep it." She put it back into the cargo pocket.

"Ready?"

"Reckon so."

The rancher lifted the old woman atop the draft and used the uphill next to the arroyo wall to clamber aboard behind her, then he urged the horse forward back into the water. In a few minutes, they passed the collapsed area, and Amy didn't seem to notice. From time to time, Rand turned to see if anyone followed.

Riding through the arroyo was deceptive. It felt safe, and it was on a long-range basis, but the chances for ambush were huge, and they continued for the better part of two hours, until the walls around them dwindled in height then became flat like the ancient seabed they entered.

They ate some of the rations he'd scavenged off the crushed flanker, and then Amy settled back into Rand's shoulder and dozed until they emerged from what was left of the diminishing arroyo.

The sun was halfway to midpoint when they hit the flats. Amy straightened up and pointed toward a large butte some six or seven miles away. The lonely formation had the appearance of a cluster of organ pipes, and it shone like polished pewter.

Rand reined the draft around, dismounted and stood on the top of a dune to have a look behind them. The landscape rose away from them to the south. There was not much to see. The desert is always still at that time of day, barring the odd rabbit or mouse or snake. By then, most wildlife has taken cover from the wicked heat and sun, underground, usually.

The desert is not truly desert. It is really arid landscape. It is populated with low trees that resemble shrubs more than trees. And these trees grow from single trunks, then sand builds up around said trunk, so in order to survive, the single trunk sprouts limbs that become roots, and sand builds up around those, and so on till the sand builds up to four or five feet with many branches. They become little islands in a sea of sand and rock, islands that provide shade, burrows, and vegetation.

From the air, the landscape can appear flat, and many a pilot has realized too late that instead of smooth terrain, the desert is actually a series of low channels, punctuated with a patchwork of uniformly high hills.

The terrain worked for the rancher. If he lay flat on the horse, he could escape detection as well as his livestock did.

Beamer was warmed up. His nature was to plod along at a steady pace, good for a draft horse, but he could lope with the best of them. "You ready for a run?" Rand asked Amy.

"Reckon we better. I will run and not be tired, walk and not faint," she replied.

The rancher kissed the air and dug his heels into the draft's sides. Beamer complied happily and broke into a steady lope, picking his way through and around the bushy dunes. He veered this way and that, right, then left, steadily navigating the sandy channels. Rand barely needed to lean one way or the other to move in the direction of the butte. The draft stayed far enough away from the vegetation so Amy would not need to draw up her legs to keep from being scratched.

The draft's smooth gait and what remained of his winter coat made the ride comfortable. Amy seemed to be having a good time. She hadn't been on a horse in decades, but she adapted well to riding bareback. The warm air flowed by, cooler than at a standstill.

Rand was edgy and would be until they found good cover. He fretted over the old woman, worrying that she was far too fragile to be on a loping horse. He judged that ten-minute's run would put them out of rifle range of men on foot. Distance over comfort, he thought, but Beamer had other ideas, and he slowed automatically to a trot when his path crossed a familiar cattle trail. Then, the draft stopped as if to question what his rider wanted to do next.

The rancher sat as high as he could to scan south along the trail to see if anyone was coming. The trail was wide enough to accommodate a vehicle like an SUV, which meant the odds were good that the intruders might use it. He saw nothing, and he swiveled his upper body around to check for trackers behind him. Again, nothing.

The air was clear, and visibility was good, usual for a spring day. Dew still glistened on the mesquite, and the dampness on the ground kept the dust from the draft's hooves to a minimum. The day would turn hot in an hour. Rand decided to chance using the trail. Neither he nor Amy had head covering; the sun would be an issue.

Rand kicked Beamer right, and the horse, sensing the eased pressure, moved onto the trail in a trot. It was his best pace. He had trained as a carriage horse and could trot for long periods without a rest, and he could cover territory at a surprising rate.

The rancher trained his eyes on the butte. In less than an hour, they reached the rocky flats that surrounded the butte. Rand dismounted and walked next to Beamer's head to guide him along the easiest path for Amy's sake. He placed the scavenged pack in front of her and reslung the AK over his shoulder.

The weapon was filthy, but the main asset of the AK was that it was dependable. It worked dirty or wet, cold or hot. Until the last decade, the rifle was the archetype guerilla warfare tool. This one had Chinese markings, relatively new. It had the urban warfare fittings: collapsible stock, polymer grips, and it could go full auto if required. Not recommended because of ammo expense, but when auto was needed, it did well for a few bursts. The problem was that it got hot and was hard to handle on auto.

The cattle trail ended at a point due south of the butte. If they proceeded directly for the base, they would have had to skirt the base a few hundred yards in the open. Rand decided to follow the sand dunes at the edge of the rock field to keep modest cover between him and any followers. Due east of the butte, he turned Beamer and made for the entrance. The party picked its way over the half mile of rock in twenty minutes without incident. For as big as Beamer was, he maneuvered easily over the rocks.

The rancher explored this area extensively when he and Carol first bought the ranch. The butte was on his property, and he discovered it by accident. Not the butte, but what the butte held. The previous owner died prior to closing of escrow, and he didn't have the time to discuss certain covenants contained in the deal, but there was one little detail that was never explained. Rand and Carol did not understand it, but they stated no objection and took possession anyway.

The seller, Tom Hamm, had insisted that the buyers not discuss with anyone anything they discovered on the property. He was kind of an eccentric old man who liked Rand immediately. In fact, Hamm told the soon to be rancher that he trusted that the buyer would honor his wishes whether the covenant was agreed to or not. He intimated that he would tell his reasons the day before escrow closed, and that if they wanted to back out, it would be okay, but Hamm asked for a non-disclosure agreement, which he never saw.

A year passed before Carol and Chuck discovered the ruins high on the side of the butte. She understood right away why Hamm wanted it kept secret. Not that all the neighbors didn't know about it. They did, but people in this area were a private bunch who minded their own business especially where "busybodies, tree-huggers, and authorities" were concerned.

Carol came home all excited, telling her husband that he was to drop everything and come with her. It being late in the day, Rand put it off until the next day, but when he saw it, he regretted not going with her that evening. When she described what she had found, he, too, understood Hamm's insistence on the covenant.

Hamm was a careful man. Before he made a decision to sell to them, he "carried" them out to all the neighbors within ten miles to make formal introductions. The word was that if any one of the neighbors were uncomfortable with Rand and Carol, the deal would have been canceled forthwith.

The neighbors were a mix of types, but they held in common the belief in privacy and individual rights. One of these was a real character name Jim Broderick, a self styled survivalist. As loud and brash as he was, his wife and two daughters were as quiet and unassuming. Rand and Carol figured he was okay because of his family and saw them occasionally in town.

After Hamm died a few days before escrow closed, Jug and Emma called on Rand and Carol and told them that they deliberately kept nosy people off their property because outsiders were nothing but problems. Carol sensed it was a "Boo Radley" thing, but thought it had more to do with privacy issues than anything else. She and Rand never suspected that it had to do with antiquities or relics, but it absolutely did.

The government had a way of taking things from these people and not paying for them. Rand's career experience confirmed it.

The day after Carol's discovery, they marched themselves to the butte and were awestruck by the cliff dwelling. They never mentioned the find to anyone, nor did Chuck, but it was not hard for him because he was home schooled and saw people outside infrequently.

The stronghold was easy to miss; Rand remembered Carol saying, as he approached the butte. The indentation into the side of the formation was hidden from view by a wide column of granite, which looked nearly separate from the main body of the butte. Between the two major formations, a steep walkable path began at the lower east base and continued upward at a little better than two to one grade until it reached a narrow flat passageway that ran ten yards before it came to a wide open space. Then there was again a small rise in elevation with a fifty-foot sheer drop on the left side, a turn to the right into the main niche.

The niche itself was situated behind the front column. It ran back fifty feet or so and was just as deep. From a small rock carved platform at the westernmost edge of the niche, the valley floor laid out like a sea of sand. The rest of the stronghold was shady until late afternoon in the winter and much of the day all summer. The granite ceiling slanted back to an eight-foot wall that curved gently to a little crevice, which sat at the fare northeast corner.

Whoever had lived there centuries earlier had built pueblo style rooms, most of which had disintegrated, but two rooms, one very large two storied affair, and another smaller room built so far away from the elements that they had survived intact down to the primeval mortar used.

The nook at the northeast corner appeared to have housed a latrine complete with an appropriate stone seating arrangement that opened to a narrow vertical drop that ended very close to the base of the butte. There were occasional openings in the shaft that permitted light and air to enter, and at the bottom, as Rand and Carol later discovered, was a fire pit. Twelfth century forced air heat complete with a narrow chimney that appeared to lead all the way to the crest of the butte.

Chapter Three

A Hole in the Wall's Just a Hole in the Wall

The sun bore down on Amy and the rancher by the time they reached the entrance to the stronghold, but cool air streamed down the passageway, refreshing them. Rand was relieved they had made it this far without being spotted. He hoped.

Beamer balked, snorted, and turned his head south, ears straight up. Rand heard gunfire, a short, rapid burst, and then another. Then silence. He lifted Amy off the horse and led her to the passageway, followed by the draft. She entered the passageway and sighed relief at the sudden cool.

"You make it up there?"

"Reckon so. He will give the feet of a deer that I might ascend to the heights," Amy answered. "But slowly."

Rand let her take a big lead before urging Beamer forward. When she was twenty feet into the cleft, the rancher clucked and the draft followed, his master trailing and holding his tail. "Walk on," he ordered, and Beamer obeyed.

The path was steeper than he remembered. Beamer picked his way forward, lunging upward at times, getting uncomfortably close to Amy, and then waiting patiently for her to proceed before he continued. They came to a wide area, and the old woman stopped to rest. The draft stamped his feet, wondering what to do, and Rand took the moment to climb the boulder for a look at the valley below.

He caught sight of someone where the cattle trail met the rock field due south of him. Rand recognized the guy as Primero who scoured the ground, looking for tracks. A moment later another joined him, then another, then seven more. They sat in the sparse shade and waited.

Rand hugged the granite, waiting to see if he'd been spotted. Probably not. He descended from his perch and urged the horse forward into the narrow passageway. Beamer was not having it. One of his sides touched a wall, and as he took a step forward, the other side touched the wall. When he tried to turn his head, it bumped the opposite wall. He balked, completely immobile.

Amy observed the situation and calmly approached the draft, taking him by the jaw and leading him forward. She was just about to lead him into the broad turn to the upper level when she stopped dead. Beamer lifted his head toward the inner niche. His rump filled the passageway opening, giving no space for Rand to pass. He wondered why everything had stopped, both here and below.

Beamer snorted his alarm snort and backed unceremoniously into Rand who fell backward. The draft backed up, trying to avoid Rand's prostrate body. He stopped, his rear legs straddling the rancher, and then Rand heard the unmistakable registration of a pump action shotgun. His blood ran cold. It was stupidity to assume no one was here already.

"Show me your hands." A male voice commanded.

Rand lay the AK aside and scooted forward between the draft's legs and used the forelegs to help himself into a sitting position.

"Come on out," the voice commanded. "Hands in front."

Amy stood staring into the niche. Rand came to his knees and peered above him to find the voice's owner.

"Holy crap, Rand. It's good to see you," It was Jim Broderick.

"We got company." Rand motioned toward the rock field. "Let me know if it's safe to bring the horse up."

Jim didn't listen. He vaulted over the rock ledge, scooped Amy up in his arms, and carried her to the interior. He returned momentarily with field glasses to the lookout ledge. Rand stood and held onto the draft, which edged toward the open area. He shied at the sheer drop to his side, so Rand stripped off his flak jacket and draped it over Beamer's head.

Jim motioned them forward, and the two ascended quickly, rounded the curve, and Rand uncovered the horse. Amy took charge of Beamer and led him into the smaller adobe room while the men shook hands.

"What about the family?" Jim asked.

"Not good. Yours?"

"Sent 'em to Phoenix last weekend." The heavyset blond man replied. "Wish I'd gone with 'em. Sorry 'bout your wife and son. Want some water?" Rand nodded, and Jim scurried off to retrieve bottles for Rand and Amy.

Rand had been more successful than he had any right to expect. If the original guys were as experienced as the ones who tracked him now, it would have been a whole different story. If they discovered the stronghold, they could stand off a hundred yards and cut them to pieces with RPGs. "Too many, Shane. Too many," echoed in his head.

Jim showing up was an asset, but not enough of a plus to make a real difference. They were in real trouble. One more body, one more set of eyes, he could come in handy. Though they'd never discussed it, Jim hinted he'd had military experience.

He sure had the weapons, which he displayed proudly while they discussed their joint predicament. Neither one could judge what was going on. They kicked around ideas, Jim's bordered on wacky. He clearly listened to too much ultra right radio. The short man had settled on "the invasion of the drug cartels." When Rand asked why, his neighbor had no real reason.

Rand's gaze drifted around the edges of the niche. Jim had apparently stocked the place well. There were a lot more provisions than could have been delivered in one trip. Apart from crates of MREs, there were a dozen five-gallon bottles of spring water, bedrolls, campstools, a camp stove, and boxes of ammunition.

Jim noticed the look over and jumped in with an explanation.

"I saw this coming…I did. So I started stocking this place months ago. Hell, you should see my cellar." His shoulders sagged. "I'd love to be there right now."

"What happened?" Rand had to ask.

"They set fire to it. Then kept shooting so I couldn't get out."

"How'd you get out?"

"I never told anybody, but I built a tunnel from my cellar to a place outside my gate. Then I built a bunker and camouflaged it. I kept a little ATV in it, and some weapons. They never saw me…. hope you don't mind me stashing stuff here."

Rand told him he appreciated it, and went to the observation point to check below while Jim took water and energy bars to Amy who had taken a place on the bedrolls near the wall. She drank the water and sat rocking back and forth humming 'Rock of Ages.'

Jim withdrew a canvas pail from his stock, went to a cistern on the west side of the niche, filled it, and took it in to the horse's quarters.

The assault group bivouacked where the cattle trail met the rock field. They rested under tarps spread over mesquite trees. They ate.

The rancher needed rest. He lay down near Amy and stared at the high, granite ceiling.

"How'd you know?" he asked Jim.

"Saw scoutin' parties come in last month. They came across, looked around, left. Not like the coyotes or drug runners. Just too weird. I called ICE, but they blew me off. Too busy, they said, to come looking for people with no drugs or who didn't stay. Then I got to thinking I should get set to defend my place."

"Why didn't you?"

"Just too damn many," he exhaled long and slow.

"What warned you?"

"I set up some IR cameras and sensors before the rains. I could see 'em comin,'" he shook his head. "I tried to call the sheriff, but they took out the cell tower right when they hit you…. I saw your place go up, and then they drove in and started on me, just like that." Jim snapped his fingers.

"You rested?" Rand asked.

"I'm okay. Go to sleep. I'll take first watch."

Rand went to the lookout point and used Jim's field glasses to scan below. The war party on the flats had wrapped up and moved east along the rock field. "Wind's changed. We'll hear 'em long before we see 'em. Got food?"

"I'm hungry." Amy stated in a matter of fact tone. The fugue was gone, and she was again an old woman with Alzheimer's.

"Yeah...yeah," the portly man hustled off into the small adobe and returned with packaged food and more water. "I've got a camp stove if you want it hot...."

Rand interrupted, "No fire right now." He was dead tired and wanted sleep. "Stay away from the lookout for now," he said as he moved to the inner wall and lay down.

Jim, meantime, pulled a canvas stool close to Amy, opened the container, and broke off pieces to feed her. She ate. "Thou preparest a table before me in the presence of mine enemies," she stated. Normally, she would have had plenty to say about the quality and quantity of the food, but now, she chewed quietly, and seemed to enjoy it. At length, she rose from her perch and stood steadily.

"I need to go to the bathroom," she announced. Jim was on his feet immediately.

"Right this way, ma'am. The old owners thought of everything," he said as he led her to an alcove where two large, flat-topped boulders, held together by gravity met and split six inches back. Jim handed her a roll of tissue and said, "I wouldn't look down if I were you."

Amy shot him the withering look only a southern woman could, making him retreat. She did look down and saw no bottom to the shaft.

When Jim returned to Rand, he asked "She any better?"

The rancher looked toward the ceiling. "'Bout the same." He motioned toward the tarp-covered cache of weapons, "What have we got?"

Jim pulled away the plastic sheet and revealed several rifles and appropriately labeled boxes of handguns. "Nothing auto...like the AK...say, where'd you get that?"

"Stole it.... this morning."

The portly man extracted an M-21. "I've got this for long range. Got it from a dealer who was a Nam vet. Then," he opened a box and pulled out a Bushmaster, pistol rigged. ". 223, but the conversion kit didn't get here in time." He opened the chamber and handed it to Rand who hefted it for balance.

"Good," he judged, and then indicating the M-21, "Can you hit anything with it?"

Jim paused for a second. "Five hundred yards, and I'm golden."

"Enough ammo?" Rand wondered if the ammo boxes were full.

"Thousand rounds per, except for the shotgun. Maybe five hundred rounds. And," Jim rose, pulled back another tarp, revealing four bales of hay. "Just in case I had to ride up here on my horse." He peeled off two flakes and took them to the adobe, which Beamer used.

Fatigue sneaked up on Rand. He lay back, feeling sore and used up. Amy had retaken her space on the bedrolls and had fallen asleep, looking like she had six or seven hours ago in the den. She snored quietly, and the calming effect of her breathing put him instantly to sleep, as well.

Jim took his place on the ledge, which overlooked the passageway. He was glad, and relieved, to have company. He wouldn't admit it, but these events frightened him badly, and he was proud of himself. The little fat guy had prepared exactly right. His family was safe in Phoenix because he had correctly interpreted the signs of impending disaster.

"They sure as hell won't laugh at me now," he thought. While it was his original intention to escape with them, he became fascinated with the attack, and his curiosity wouldn't let him leave. That and the normal belief that what was happening wasn't really possible. Most victims can't believe terrible things are happening until it is too late. It's what happened to Jim.

His survivalist game converted to a deadly reality before he knew it. He was luckier than most. His neighbors were tough, hard-bitten westerners who were likely caught flat-footed by the assault. Although Jim had created a good stockpile, he never believed for a minute he'd have to use it. Like many survivalists, the preparations were mere one-up-manship played out in cafes and social events and on the Internet.

"Off by a week," he mused to himself. Disbelief works that way. No one was more surprised than he when his computer alarms woke him to the infrared pictures on the screen.

The SUVs tripped the sensors on the road exit to his place. The first alert occurred at 11:30, way past his bedtime, but he'd wanted to see the late news from Los Angeles. He dashed off notes to friends and like-minded folks around the country when the first alarm came on screen.

Jim toggled over to the camera mounted on the wind tower, panned and zoomed toward the southwest coordinate preprogrammed into the computer control. He scanned back and forth till he found movement.

It was normal to see the illegals and drug runners stop to pick up contraband, but he'd never seen them so close to his place. They liked desolate areas. This time he saw four SUVs stopped on the highway next to his road and a dozen more lined up along the highway, running dark. The IR picked up the hot engines, tires, and bodies inside them.

He zoomed in for a closer look and relaxed a bit when he saw ICE insignia on the doors. Jim surmised it had to be a Fed operation, and he was glad they were finally doing something about the border situation. He was well acquainted with local law enforcement that had informed him that they were too overworked and too underequipped to stop the incursions.

Jim decided he'd better get dressed in case his place was needed for assistance. He shuffled into fatigues and toggled around to his various cameras to see if he could get a line on the folks' activities. Eventually, more SUVs showed up, and he could detect a group at the front of one vehicle going over what looked like a map.

He settled into his desk chair and dozed, not meaning to, but this stuff was pretty boring. Jim had seen it all before. Not this close, but it was nothing to report back to his Internet buddies. He'd wait.

At 1:15, he was startled from his dozing by one of the alarms. His screen was in standby mode, so he clicked it awake. Now, all the SUVS but four were on the move. The passengers from the static vehicles retrieved gear and weapons and began to don personal armor. Jim rapidly toggled to another, lower-based camera that focused on his road.

He saw two groups of ten approach his driveway some 150 yards from the house where he sat. The men milled around, talking and looking at their watches. "Must be some big operation," he muttered and wondered why he'd gotten no heads up from the authorities. He guessed it was too hush-hush for anybody unofficial to be in the loop.

The clock on his computer said it was 1:30, and another alarm burped to life. Jim checked to see which camera came to life on the motion sensor. It was the one midpoint on his driveway. Eight men in battle dress moved up the hill toward the house. Another burp and a camera near the barn intruded on the screen. Then another one came on, a total of four cameras were scanning his property. He toggled back to the tower camera, switched to full infra red and panned his property.

Aside from the eight on the road, four moved east toward his barn, another four circled west into the meadow, near the water tank. He tilted up to see the other four get into the SUVs. The men on the ground moved casually, not like any assault team he'd ever seen, but he felt the adrenaline make its slow crawl up his neck.

"See.... see," he exclaimed at the screen. "By God, I was right. See..." His satisfaction froze in his throat when the enormity of the situation rested on him. "This can't be good," he said out loud. He raced for his gun cabinet and pulled out the shotgun. The computer burped again, and the camera that overlooked his garage and parking area showed on the screen. He dithered for a moment wondering if he should send out an attack alert, but before he could do anything, the lights went out.

The computer had a power-safe on it, but the screen went blank, then the words "No Signal" appeared. He was too late, and that was when an incendiary device broke through the dining room window, followed by another through the bedroom window, and another through the den window where he stood.

The resulting fire was instantaneous. Jim could only think of getting out. He ran to the broken window to escape the flames, but gunfire opened up from the front yard sending him to the floor. He heard more gunfire and saw his front door splinter. The portly rancher crawled to the bedroom behind the kitchen and lifted the carpet to expose the cellar door.

His hand found the battery-operated light and switched it on. Smoke filled the room. He descended quickly and pulled the concrete lined door closed behind him. Jim was scared. He couldn't think.

His first thought was to sit tight. The cellar was a bombproof concrete-lined bunker. It would be safe enough to hold him until help came, but what if it didn't come? He had built the place for his family to use, but they were already away; he had to decide, and he opted to escape.

The noise of the fire above was deafening. The air in the cellar was close. Jim opened the little hatch at his left hand and crawled through, closing the hatch behind him. He prayed there were no snakes in here.

It took fifteen minutes to crawl the two hundred yards to the escape bunker. It was hard work, and he wished he'd taken the time to build it tall enough to walk through. Jim crawled over the equipment he'd stored in the past months. He regretted not keeping it neat. In a few minutes, he cleared a small path in the little room and pressed the double doors open.

The landscape was lit from behind him by his burning house. He didn't want to look, but he had to see if there were any intruders near him. During his crawl to the bunker, the SUVs had moved near the house. He counted twelve at the house and checked around for anyone near him. Satisfied that he had space, Jim rolled his little four-wheeler out onto the wash that fronted the bunker. He checked his holster for his Colt and push started the ATV.

Jim was a gadget guy, and his wife hated the noise the ATV made, so he mounted a huge muffler to cut the noise. Tonight, he was glad he did.

He dared not go to the highway. The only path left to him was down the wash and onto the desert floor. There was enough fuel to make it as far north as the big highway, then to help, but that was as risky as going south. Jim remembered that the stronghold was provisioned, he knew the way, and could find it in the dark. He looked over his shoulder to check for followers, and he saw a fireball in the direction of Rand and Carol's house, and another glow at Jug and Emma's, then, he heard the report of the explosion at Rand's place.

Jeez, he thought. This is bad.

Jim rode on into the darkness trying to figure out what was happening. He went north for an hour and turned right toward the rock field that lay fifteen minutes ahead. He spent the ride calculating how many men he'd seen. Twelve SUVs with five apiece. Sixty. What if there were more?

The assault looked pro. Hitting three places, taking out a cell tower, cutting lines. Had to be more. Had to be. The attack was coordinated.

When he sensed he was near the rock field, he ran the ATV up on a brushy dune, dismounted, and cut branches to lay over it. He kept one free and went down the little hill, brushing the sand to remove the wheel ruts from the sand. He was done in minutes and he tossed the branch onto another brushy dune.

Crossing the rock field was nerve racking. He heard gunfire in the distance, but as far as he was concerned it was right next-door. Jim made it to the passageway of the stronghold, and when he made it to the top, he plunged his head into the nearest cistern, dried off, and then he slept, awakening before sunup.

Jim scanned the distance with his field glasses and saw three armed men in fatigues hurrying east. He could not identify them and figured they were chasing someone. He did not know who. He scanned back toward his place and saw nothing but residual smoke drifting east and mingling with the smoke from his neighbor's place. It scared him.

The portly rancher wanted to go back and do something to those guys, but he dared not move from cover till he had a handle on what was happening. He paced for an hour.

He went to his lookout ledge and scanned again. This time he saw a draft horse on the cattle trail carrying double. He recognized Rand and the old woman who lived with him. Jim considered signaling them, but checked himself, not wanting to be seen by any of the bad guys. Although he wanted to run down the passageway out onto the rock field, he couldn't reveal his presence on the risk that the two might be followed.

It was a relief when the horse turned east. Going to the next ranch was the best idea for a man who was responsible for an old woman. Jim let his guard down and dozed until he heard sounds coming from the passageway. If he had to make a last stand, he would make it here.

Jim was relieved when Rand appeared from behind the big draft horse. Although they'd never talked about the past, the portly man knew the look of a man with a big past. Rand had the look of a man with kept secrets, a man who'd seen very bad things, maybe had done some of those bad things. He remembered the old saw about there being rough men who do hard things so the rest of us can sleep safe.

Rand woke to a clap of thunder and came to his feet quickly very like the old days. The day had turned to late afternoon. He turned to seek Amy and found her sitting on the bedroll exactly as she was when he went to sleep. The old woman sat utterly still on the bedroll. She was awake, but she had the 1000-yard stare. Nobody home in there.

It was warm yet. A breeze lifted from the south where thunderheads overtook the butte on wings of freshening air. The rain was on its way, and it would erase any trace of his and Amy's flight. Keeping low, he crept to the lookout for a good vantage point on the valley floor. He glanced at Jim's sleeping form next to the berm, opted not to wake him. He wanted the field glasses still wrapped around the other man's neck, but the silence of the moment felt right.

Rand looked over the top of the lookout, checking first the cattle trail, then the rock field. He detected movement out in the shadow of the storm clouds. He nudged Jim, rousing him. He put his finger to his lips and pointed outside the stronghold.

Startled to wakefulness and abashed at sleeping on his watch, the portly man rose as if to stand, but Rand pulled him to his knees, calming him with a pat. He held out his hand and whispered "Glasses," which Jim relinquished. Rand lay on his chest on the slant that led to the lookout and looked through the lenses.

There was activity, all right. Several men had found the cattle trail and followed it toward the butte. Moments later, several more appeared out of the dunes and joined the leading group.

"Well, crap…" Rand spit.

Jim looked askance, and Rand responded, "For a minute or so, I thought mighta beat 'em."

Jim took the glasses and peered out, at Rand's direction, to where the band rallied. They were about a mile and a half away when they fanned out like a search party. They took care to search each brushy dune as they went. It did not look like an assault team.

Rand checked the sky, noticing an advancing squall line that would overtake them in a short time. Good, he thought. This might work. The stronghold could be safe for the moment, but he held no illusion that they would not return. Anyone interested enough to send out a search party for people who were probably dead, or would die out here, was a serious contender. It didn't make sense, but it was an indication of the gravity of the situation.

The two men backed away from the lookout and moved to better cover.

"What do you think?" Jim asked.

"We better get a plan." Rand said. "And I need some food."

Jim hurried into the adobe and returned with water, biscuits, and jerky. While Rand ate, he questioned Jim about the depth of how he'd stocked the stronghold. There was enough food for six adults for two months if it were properly rationed. There were weapons for four, ammo for sustained firefights, and water that replenished every other day in this season.

It was an impressive amount of work. Jim had also concealed pitons and carabiners at strategic points both inside and outside the stronghold. He had hidden a climbing rope that began in the latrine and terminated at the very top of the butte, somewhere Rand had never been.

This particular butte was rather unimpressive when compared to others farther to the north. This unimpressive nature was probably why the cliff dwellings had never been discovered by federal or state explorers.

For openers, the butte sat near the middle of an ancient seabed, surrounded by many deep canyons that ran as much as a quarter mile off the main bed. The seabed was bordered by nearly vertical walls in most places, much like Rand's ranch site. Most of the walls were capped by loose limestone outcroppings, making them appear to be mesas, which they were not. If followed, the "mesas" would have been shown to be a continuous serrated line that met up somewhere. From the air, the footprint area resembled more a gigantic amoeba rather than a series of mesas.

The butte itself was a piece of granite, which rose more than a hundred feet off the rock field. Like an advanced design building, the foot print was reminiscent of a flattened oval, running two hundred yards along the north and south face, and short of a hundred yards along the east and west faces. Its rugged sides were so defined that no pieces had fallen off since its prehistoric formation when the rock field came to be, and it did have the form and appearance of a pipe organ if viewed through squinted eyes. The south face was as smooth as the other faces were not. From the base halfway up, a large rock appeared to be a titan's thumb emerging from the rock field, and on the side of the butte was a corresponding "thumbprint" the stronghold hid, obscured by the "thumb."

Rand returned to the lookout and watched the search party move slowly toward them, following the track of the draft. He gauged their pace and compared it with the velocity of the oncoming storm. If he were correct, the storm would arrive at the rock field before the search party did.

A lightning strike and the subsequent thunderclap to the south halted the group. They continued forward albeit haltingly. Rand picked out the leader and recognized him as the little guy from last night, Primero, who emerged from the center knot of men and gesticulated forcefully. The others were less excited about being there than he. They did not want to be out in the open in a thunderstorm.

The little man stopped and spoke into a communications device, probably a walkie-talkie, and the group suddenly lost its tension. They proceeded back the way they came and met up with one of the SUVs coming down the cattle trail, bouncing up and down like a Conestoga wagon.

The vehicle was well rigged with running boards so those who did not fit inside clung to the luggage racks and stood on the running boards. The SUV came about and sped up the trail into the squall line, leaving Primero, who refused to go, under a tarp next to the cattle trail.

Rand sighed heavily and rolled over to face Jim and Amy.

"Dodged the bullet there, eh?" Jim stood and stretched.

"They'll be back," Rand, breathed deep the smell of desert under rain.

"Why?"

"Strategic reason, I dunno. Tactically, they want to see the bodies," Rand dropped his head slightly. "For them to send a whole team out was a big deal. They have to know we're all dead."

Jim made no reply for a minute. "What are we gonna do?"

"We can't outrun 'em'? That's for sure. And if we stay here, they will absolutely find us," he said flatly. "They'll come back after the rain. They could follow the other trail to the other ranch, but my guess is that they have people over there already. The only place to look is here."

Jim paced toward the adobe and back. "If we fight, they'll just send more."

"It would chew up time. Maybe time they don't have," Rand postulated. "This operation can't stay secret for long. If we give them enough grief…delay them. Give ICE and maybe the National Guard enough time to get here. We might just survive."

"How long can we hold 'em off from here?" Jim fidgeted.

"We can't." Rand made his decision.

Chapter Four

Someone didn't get the memo

Rand uncovered hay bales and took them one by one into the small adobe. Jim followed along, helping where he could. The ranchers set the bales near the wall, leaving an alcove near the south wall. After making Amy stand, the moved the bedrolls in for a place for her.

The rain fell fiercely bringing little rivulets from the outer wall across the sloping ceiling of the niche into the cisterns. Rand had to admire the ancients who had designed the place. They moved the rest of the supplies except the weapons and ammo into the little adobe near Beamer.

He turned to Jim. "I'm going to draw their fire. Don't even look till you hear it set up."

He crept to the lookout. "Set up here. Fire no more than three times, then move away fast. Count to twenty, no matter what you see. Count to twenty, then come back, set up a little different, then take three. Got it?"

Jim nodded.

"If they return fire, go down the path a little way. You'll be safe there. If you hear them coming, use the shotgun. Then get next to Amy as fast as you can. Behind the hay."

"Okay." Jim was visibly shaken. He said nothing as they led Amy into her cubbyhole.

Rand wanted to be encouraging, but things didn't look so good from his angle either. He lied. "We can do this." Then with a laugh, he said "Just make sure you don't shoot me, okay?"

Jim didn't take it as a joke, and Rand said seriously, "Look, Jim, this may not be a war, but it's as close as we're gonna get. Shoot 'em in the back if you have to." He patted Jim on the shoulder. "I'm depending on you."

Rand looked outside into the late afternoon. The storm had legs. The rain was thick and driven. The winds were fierce. It was time to go.

The rancher took a pair of cargo pants from Jim's stock and put them on. He found a pair of tennis shoes that fit and laced them up tight. He borrowed Jim's ammo belt and hunting jacket and loaded it with ammo. Rand checked the M-15, and made sure the mags were clean, loaded, and ready. He put the spare magazines for the Sig in his cargo pockets and strapped the pistol inside the hunting jacket. He found a spare sheath and laced it onto his right leg.

He was as ready as he could get considering his present situation.

The rancher crept to the lookout and checked Primero on the flats. The little man stubbornly sat in the rain, occasionally peering out from under his tarp. "Gotta admire his dedication," Rand murmured.

The rancher, followed by his neighbor, went to the latrine, let some of the rope above down and began his descent. He chose this avenue because the way he came in was exposed to Primero's position. This exit was unpleasant because of the late usage, but Rand figured "What the hell, if they kill me they won't want to touch me."

It wasn't as awful as he expected. The heavy rainwater sluiced through the chute pretty well. It beat rice paddies. In five or six minutes, he was ten feet from the opening at the base of the butte's northeast corner, well out of sight of the lone sentry. He was soaked through.

Rand edged down the last distance wedging him feet on one side, and the butte on the other. At last, he was outside. He couldn't see anything to the south, so he had no idea as to the progress of the storm. It still poured where he stood, and he wanted the cover, but he was now committed. The rancher headed west along the north face of the butte and made the two hundred yards quickly.

His plan was to cross the rock field out of sight of Primero, to make it into the desert proper, and to circle around to a point between the little man and up the cattle trail; but when he made the turn to the south, Rand heard the sound of machinery, like a semi rig off to the west. No, not a semi. This sounded like a tank.

The rancher sprinted, as best he could on the rocky terrain, toward the sound. He cleared the field and mounted a dune for a better look. The rain fell in sheets obscuring his vision. In fact, the rain was so heavy that Rand almost ran into what he believed to be an outrider guard. So intent on finding the source of the noise, the rancher jogged between the dunes and suddenly spotted out the corner of his eye, a tall, heavily armed man coming toward him.

The guard was so busy wiping the rain off his face that he missed Rand's duck and cover. The guard walked past the rancher's hiding place under a scrub tree, close enough for Rand to touch. After the guard passed, the rancher climbed to the top of the nearest dune and had a look.

A quarter of a mile away, a large track mounted skip loader toiled along a wide arroyo. Half a block behind, a track-mounted crane, probably a twenty-tonner, followed the original's trace. Behind the crane, a flat bed semi lurched along, skidding and slipping in the machine packed sand of the arroyo. Rand expected and saw another outrider guard following the path of the man he'd nearly bumped into.

He ducked away before he could see what was on the flat bed, but he did make out a large camouflaged box. The rancher backed away thinking, 'this can't be good.' His instinct was to follow this group, but the first priority was to protect the stronghold and its occupants.

Rand broke away and jogged due south to bring himself where he had planned. What he saw bothered him, reminded him of something. The machinery really bothered him. He decided that this whole shootin' match was not drugs, not people smuggling, and he wondered where everybody else was.

In five minutes, the rancher arrived at the cattle trail, a few hundred yards south of Primero. The rain let up as quickly as it had begun, leaving a rainbow to the east. It was still and quiet. He was glad to be downwind when he heard behind him the sound of a SUV barreling along the cattle trail coming in his direction. It halted briefly, and then sped along until Rand could see a glare from the roof. He scrambled through brush up the slope of the nearest dune and found himself in a clear area ten feet across.

The mesquite provided good cover all the way around him. It was one of those lairs used by either antelope or coyotes between foraging or raiding. There were low openings on four sides that animals had used to get inside.

Rand knelt and waited for the SUV to pass, and he was glad he did. Another vehicle followed close. Both carried men inside and outside in the same manner as he had seen them leave earlier in the day. Through the foliage he tried to get a count, but they passed by so abruptly, he could only surmise.

Counting Primero, the rancher calculated six inside and four outside each SUV, coming to a total of twenty-one. Not good. If one man stayed with each vehicle, there were still nineteen to deal with in one way or the other.

The SUVs halted, Rand believed, at the edge of the rock field. It was a lead pipe cinch they weren't willing to risk the undercarriages on that terrain. This gave rise to the thought that the SUVs would be needed later. If not, these guys would have risked the damage.

The late afternoon sun broke through the western edges of the sky, golden shafts streaming in a low angle over the landscape and prominently illuminating the butte and turning it red and gold in the trailing squall line that swept north and east. The rancher saw the bare western edge of the stronghold. There was no movement on the lookout.

Rand turned his plan over in his mind. The SUVs were unexpected. His original thought was to hit and run, now he had to deal with the vehicles first to partially cripple the assault. If these guys were any good, sentries would stay with the vehicles, one would anyway. He hoped it was one sentry.

It struck Rand odd that he should give a damn about these guys. There was nothing to keep him here. Carol and Chuck were gone. Amy was pretty old. How much life did she have left? Jim had taken his chances, and they had cost him. Why should he risk it when he could run, probably make it out and call the authorities? Hell, he didn't even have any friends to fight for, which is what they always say about combat...you fight for your friends.

Nope. There was no real good reason to fight this fight, cut and dried. He wasn't fighting for his country, not that he knew of. So that was it. He thought for a minute because there would be no time to think later. Then, he decided.

Rand would fight because these bastards were bullies and because they just plain pissed him off. They were doing it because they *could* do it. The government had turned itself into a bunch of eunuchs, and these guys were taking the advantage for purposes he did not yet know. But the rancher did not need to know the end game, he knew the right-now game, and he didn't like it.

He had faced death before. Rand was not remotely regretful for the killing of the men at the house. It was a sure case of kill or be killed; but now, he was the hunter. Stalking and killing is a cold business, like playing pool. Get excited and you make mistakes, he thought as he let the anger inside cool.

The sun lodged on the horizon, and it was time to move. The rancher crawled out of his blind and moved north carefully on a route parallel to the cattle trail in and out along the sand. When he judged that he was in line with the parked SUVs he went as close to the edge of the rock field as he dared to gauge the opposition.

Several intruders had entered the field, negotiating the boulders between the desert bed and butte with care. He counted eight in the field. These did not look behind themselves, focused only ahead. He edged farther and counted eight more who trod the sandy boundary. That left three at the SUVs. Rand backtracked south twenty yards and peeked up over the mesquite to check his first opponents' positions.

He was in luck. The driver of the first SUV sat in the back seat watching a video. Another paced near the back of the other SUV, looking like he needed to relieve himself. There should have been one more. The rancher peered south. Nothing. Maybe, the other one was on the other side of the vehicles. He didn't

like it, but the pacer moved in his direction unzipping
his pants, so he had to make his move.

Rand shrank back slightly, pulled his assault knife,
and waited. The pacer turned south and began to
relieve himself on the next scrub tree. The rancher
lunged low and caught the guy midstream. He
jammed the knife up under the man's ribs with his
right hand and slid his left up his back and around his
jaw to silence him. His quarry slumped toward the
ground, and the rancher bore his weight till his body
came to rest.

Rand rolled the body onto its back, removed the
knife, and wiped it clean on the man's pants. He
looked at the dead man's face and got the shock of
his life. This guy didn't look Latin at all. He was dark
all right, but he had a full beard, and he wore a white
and red scarf. And he smelled odd, not garlicky like a
Latin.

He had no time to consider the oddity. The light was
going, and so was he.

Rand moved toward the SUVs. He saw the video
screen down and playing some movie.
The left backdoor was open, and he saw a combat
boot dangling casually near the ground. He wondered
where the last guy was, but there was no time to
worry about him.
He picked up a pebble and tossed it at the boot. It
shook, but nothing followed.

Rand tossed another, and the man came out of the
SUV, annoyed that he'd been interrupted. The
rancher leapt forward and smacked the enemy against

the door, stepped back, and slammed the door against the man who fell into the corner of the door and car body. The rancher slammed the butt of his knife into the man's forehead. Done.

He checked the body. This one was Latin.

Rand ducked around to the other side of the SUV to search for the last man. There was no one. He dropped to his knees under the first SUV and drove the knife into the gas tank, one on the bottom, and the other at the fill hose. He rolled over, came to his feet and ran to the back of the other vehicle. He performed the same operation on this SUV and stood away a few feet to check to see the flow of the uphill meet the flow of the downhill SUV.

When the two streams met, Rand lit a match and tossed it toward the pool under the uphill SUV. He immediately turned east and sprinted into the desert. Fifteen seconds later the vehicle fire flared behind him, but he was long gone by a hundred yards.

Rand ran a path that curved north, and as he expected, the rock field group of eight turned and ran toward the fire. It was the perfect time for Jim to open up, but nothing happened. The rancher let the boundary crew slide past him in single file, then he knelt on the sand and laced off six shots that found their marks, more or less. He counted four probable kills and two woundeds before he sprinted south into the desert.

The ten left returned fire to where they believed the assault came, but Rand had already moved back to the cattle trail south of the burning vehicles. He fired twice more, scoring two hits. He didn't know how good the hits were.

He chanced crossing the cattle trail, exposing himself to a few auto salvos, which missed. This time he arced northwest, hoping to draw them into better position for Jim on the lookout. Rand was at the point of congratulating himself for the up-to-now success of his raid when a round whistled past him. He wondered where it had come from because he heard no report. He ducked left and hit the deck. Another slug slammed into the sand two feet in front of him, and he heard the characteristic spit of a silenced weapon. Whoever fired on him, fired from the south, and he was close enough and high enough to see the rancher.

Rand rolled under a mesquite and waited.

There's smart, and then, there's real smart. The man who fired on Rand was rear guard…and good. Smart enough to be patient, hide, and wait. Really, this guy was smart enough to pin him down and wait for the other bad boys to find him. Where was Jim?

The voices of the other bad boys drifted toward him from the north. Rand assessed his situation. Nine or so north. One, albeit well hidden and good, to the south. He guessed the silencer guy would not use the cattle trail. This guy would take the dunes as quickly as possible, staying high, and that meant the others would not take a chance of hitting their boy.

Rand would have to make the silencer guy make a mistake. The game went from pool to tennis.

It was almost dark, but that meant zip. If the guy had a silencer, he was also IR equipped, real A-team material, and Rand had not forgotten that the guys who came into his house were equipped exactly this way. This guy was cold, too. Rand hoped his assailant was still playing pool.

The rancher lifted to a crouch and ran as due west as the terrain would allow. He skirted close to the mesquite without touching them. The damp sand was good for running. Rand was not tired, but he kept wondering about Jim as he ran. It was a mistake.

Something red glinted in his left eye, and he knew immediately what it was. He dropped instantly to the ground, but it was too late. Something hit him on the left side of his forehead as he went down. It didn't knock him out, but it certainly blurred his vision. Rand fell face forward on his rifle. He couldn't move.

Chapter Five

Dead is one thing, really dead's another

He lay still in the darkness for a few minutes. His strength was gone out of him. When he opened his eyes, one eye saw dark fluid; the other couldn't see anything because the blood covered it. He heard footfalls coming toward him. Only one set. Rand stiffened, waiting for one more shot.

It never came. "Allahu akbar, asshole," came the words from the shooter. Rand felt a boot kick him over onto his back. He let himself go slack, hoping this would be the shooter's mistake.

It was.

The man walked north and called out to his comrades in broken Spanish, then he called out in what Rand recognized as a middle-eastern language. In Spanish, he ordered some to continue the search, but the others were apparently told to join him and go back the way they came.

The shooter ordered the Latins to bury Rand's body and any others they might find. The rancher stayed absolutely still, and the shooter and two more headed south.

Nothing like a smug sniper, Rand thought. With three leaving, he had six bad boys who believed he was dead. He lay motionless for what seemed hours but was actually only a few minutes. Two of his assailants ambled over to where he lay and, using military surplus shovels, began to dig a small trench very close to him. They threw his rifle to the side, one remarking that he should get the rifle, the other agreeing, provided he could have whatever else they found on the body.

The burial detail made a fist bump close to him and congratulated each other on their good fortune and on the fact that the rancher had been killed. The digging in the sand was easy, and they weren't going deep, so they were quite relaxed as they worked, chatting it up. At one point, Rand was ready to make his move, but the conversation turned gossipy about what they were doing.

One man, called Guerrero by the other, mentioned he was ready to go home to his wife that he didn't want to be within five hundred miles of the border when it happened. The other, called Prensa said they would be okay a mere hundred miles south, that the "bomba" would only work over a five hundred mile radius. Guerrero asked how far it was to Nebraska.

The conversation was interrupted by an angry order to hurry the job, so they ramped up their speed. Rand had heard enough. When they picked him up to drop him in the shallow trench, he had time to reach inside the hunting jacket for the Sig. his thumb found the safety before they could react, and he fired one round into the eye of the man who held his feet. The guy fell backward, letting the rancher's feet drop. The other tried to get a hold on the rancher's neck, so Rand stuck the muzzle of the Sig under the man's shirt and pulled the trigger.

Once again, blood went everywhere. He staggered to his feet, looking through one eye to find the rifle in the dark. The rancher heard men running, stumbling in the rock field. Although he was a mere thirty yards from the rocky ground, he decided he could not hold off four motivated men in his present condition. He ditched the idea of finding the rifle and ran for the cattle trail.

As he sprinted away from his grave, Rand glanced toward the stronghold. It was lit up like a Christmas tree. He heard a call from near the rock field and two of his assailants broke off the chase and ran back toward the rock field. This left one man in his pursuit.

Finally, he thought. Rand gained some ground on his pursuer and vaulted as best he could onto the top of a dune and waited. He was still bleeding from his forehead. Maybe it had stopped for a while, he didn't know. He drew his knife and cut a strip out of the hunting jacket, one long enough to tie around his head, hoping it would stop the blood long enough to let him see with both eyes.

He was thirsty, but he dared not seek water until the pursuer was out of the way. Dammit, he thought. Where was Jim?

The pursuer came within twenty feet, and by his breathing, Rand could tell the man was as exhausted as he was. The man called out "Senor Rand, come out. I won't hurt you. You are my friend. You were always good to me. I will let you go. I don't like these guys." The rancher knew the voice. It was Misael, one of his seasonal roundup guys, and he nearly stood up to reveal himself, but he stopped short.

"I'm sorry about Senora Carol and the boy…"
Suddenly, the rancher remembered last night when he
heard a voice he thought he recognized. It made
sense. The assault party knew the layout of the house,
the whole ranch.

"I don't know why the house burned. It wasn't
s'posed to burn," he called out.

Rand got it. They needed a staging area. They burned
everybody else out within twenty miles, but his place
was useful.

Misael grew frustrated. "You might as well come out,
my friend. We're going to take it all back anyway.
Muy pronto. Viva Aztlan. You can't win, gabacho."
He trudged closer to Rand's hiding place. He was so
close the rancher could hear him wheeze.

Rand wiped the blood away from his eye and stood
facing Misael's back. "Aztlan, my ass," he rasped
and he shot Misael through the neck.

From the rock field someone shouted "Estufo,
Misael? Matelo?"

"Si, lo mate," Rand tried to mimic Misael's voice,
saying that yes, he had killed the man.

Rand hopped through the mesquite clump and went
to Misael's body and felt around to find anything
useful. The rancher located a canteen, opened it, and
drank greedily. He poured some on his hand and
splashed it on his face. It helped, but his left eye still
bothered him.

Rand ran his hand over the wound and found a large swelling above his left eye. The bandage held, but his head hurt as bad as he'd ever hurt. He wished for an ampoule, not caring if it didn't work for a head wound. He bent back down and found a rifle, another AK. He checked the magazine, half full. There were two more in an ammo pouch, which he lifted from the corpse.

Rand finished the water, looking toward the stronghold. There was more light coming from the niche than a campfire or camp stove would provide. Not good. He didn't know how much he had left in him, but there was nothing else he could do.

He started toward the rock field. It wasn't easy. He hurt, could barely see, and didn't know what lay ahead. He did know that there were three men out there, and that he was sure he hadn't killed Primero. When Rand came to the rock field, he heard the three marauders stumbling across the field. From the sound of it, they were at least two thirds of the way across it.

Since they believed the rancher to be Misael, Rand did not have to move in stealth mode. He picked up the pace as best he could. It was too dark to make out exactly where they were, so he dared not chance firing an auto salvo. Thirty rounds don't last long if you don't know where they're going. He needed to be on top of them.

The assailants appeared to know where they were going. That bastard must have told them about the cliff dwellings, he thought, but he was distracted momentarily by a sound that drifted toward him. It was a faraway sound like something he'd heard along the DMZ in Nam. He stopped for a moment and scanned the northwest horizon and saw a glow of artificial light over a canton. He was positive the sound emanated from that point, but there was no time to investigate.

Rand had crossed two thirds of the field when he saw flashlights flick on near the entranceway to the passage. He drew up the AK to fire, but it was too late. All three men had disappeared behind the boulder. The light cast on the boulder perfectly outlined the bodies. It was the right moment. He hurried forward, forgetting the pain and exhaustion.

When he arrived at the entrance, Rand peered around the edge to get a bead on the assailants. One stood near him, a few yards away, facing upward. Another was halfway up, and he spotted Primero at the turn that led to the big open space. He shouted toward the interior in English. "Drop it.... now." The rancher heard metal strike stone. There was only one conclusion, Jim had surrendered.

Rand fired twice into the back of the man nearest him, and that man fell forward. The other turned instantly and fired a burst, full auto toward him. The rancher ducked back in time to let the rounds pass harmlessly and glance off the boulders in the field.

He dropped to a prone position and scrunched toward the opening once more. He used the dark background to hide his position. The man above fired another salvo, but the slugs went high, passing feet above Rand's head. He spider lunged forward while clicking full auto. He snapped off eight or nine rounds, and his target fell, tumbling toward him.

When the rancher came to his feet, he saw that Primero had taken cover beyond the rim of the stronghold. Rand was about to cross the bodies of the two dead men in the passageway when the guy he'd just shot scrambled to his feet and charged the rancher. Rand reacted quickly, firing low and walking the rounds from crotch to head. It did the job, but the weapon was empty. He backed away, searching his pockets for another magazine. He had either dropped them on the field, when he hit the deck. Either way, he was out of ammo, and the weapons of the two he'd just killed were out of reach and exposed.

Sounds of a struggle up above. Rand heard an unmistakable thud and knew someone had gotten hit in the head. He took the opportunity to climb over the bodies and make it up the passageway to the point where it narrowed. He peeked around the outcropping of granite just in time to see a short weapon like a Mac 10 appear over the edge. Rand shoved his back into the wall a second before the weapon fired a full magazine down the passageway. He heard the mag latch click, then in short order, another re-engaged. There was not enough time to get to the dead men's weapons.

He was stuck, and Primero knew it.

"You should come out now, or I will kill your friend," Primero spoke in perfect English, no hint of a Spanish accent. If there was an accent, it wasn't Spanish.

"Go ahead...he means nothing to me," Rand answered. "I'll just wait you out, and kill you when you come down."

"You have no time, friend. My people will come for me when I don't come back. You have nothing," he boasted. "We killed everybody, and your police and the federal people won't come. We have them busy elsewhere. You are alone."

Primero had an ego. Rand would give him that. The Mac came over the rim and spent another magazine; scattering rock chips in every direction.

"You still there, Mister Bad Man?" Primero shouted. "How long you going to stay down there? Come on up and face me like a man."

The rancher fretted for a moment about Amy, but he figured it was possible she was sitting in her cubbyhole unaware of what was happening outside. Odds were good that Jim was dead. Rand wouldn't shed many tears over his loss, useless bastard. Again, there was the sound of a mag latch and another of mag engagement.

"Don't worry, old man," Primero mocked. "I have plenty of ammunition. I'm not like these stupid spics. I don't shoot at shadows."

That was interesting. Rand decided to play on this guy's ego. "Nobody's coming for you. You're not important enough...."

Primero fired another burst. "That's what you think. I've been with this from the very beginning, kafir."

"Oh, riiiight," Rand answered, his voice echoing off the ceiling of the niche.

"You know nothing, you are a fool like all Americans. We will destroy you in the blink of an eye. You won't even know what hit you." Primero fired a short burst. "You will have no warning."

"You think you are the only ones with remote weapons, with drones, hah," he laughed raucously. "We will do what we want when we want, and you have no defense."

Rand spoke back intensely "Big talk for a loser who's stuck on a rock."

"I have a hostage. I did not kill your friend."

"He's not my friend. He's your liability."

"I don't believe you. You Americans fear death. You don't want him to die. You want to save him. I know how you think. I lived in this country for years. I know you," he talked on. "And I know you desert people. No, my friend, you don't want him to die."

Primero was right. Rand did not want Jim to die, and he was very concerned for the old woman. He heard the gunman move and saw by the shadows that his opponent was readying to descend the passageway, but not alone. Rand heard Jim groan, sounding as if he were being forced to his feet. The shadows confirmed the rancher's suspicions. His enemy was finally impatient. The rancher knew he had gotten under Primero's skin.

He ventured a glance out and saw the little man behind the portly Jim, pushing him forward. If Rand moved out and fled, he was cannon fodder. If he fired, hitting Jim was going to happen. Primero was so small, hitting his legs wasn't an option, and he would kill Jim as he went down.

The little man fired a few rounds down the passageway, which were meant to back Rand off, but the rancher noticed that the little man fired like a gangbanger, the grip sideways. It looked tough, but it was nuts. Macs specifically tended to jam that way because the ejectors were designed to eject sideways, not vertically, especially when they were hot, and this weapon had rapped off three or fours mags in the past few minutes.

Rand looked out to draw fire, and Primero obliged him with a burst. The little man moved slowly under the weight of Jim who tried to cooperate as well as a man roused from a kayo could. Rand looked out again. Primero fired again and drew closer to the trapped rancher.

Rand gauged that Primero and his captive had reached the wide place in the passageway by the sound of the pair scraping through the brass casings that had fallen from the rim when he fired his scattershot salvos. Rand stuck his head out once more, and the little man fired once, and the weapon jammed. The rancher seized the opportunity, charging straight up the passageway.

Primero shoved Jim toward Rand and backed up the path, tugging at the register, trying to unjam the Mac. Rand shoved Jim aside and charged up toward a now fleeing Primero. Since the little man was on level footing, he was able to cross the niche halfway by the time he had cleared the jam. He turned, firing as he pivoted, his rounds running into the night. Then, the little man stopped firing and let his weapon hand drop to his side.

Rand stopped his charge, knowing that the little man was no danger any more. Primero stood for a moment, turned his face to the left, and rested his gaze on Amy who stood in the opening of the adobe, a-smoking 380 in her outstretched hand. She held the weapon pointed at Primero's head and followed it down until the little man crumpled to his knees, the flat on the granite floor of the stronghold.

The shots she fired were lost in the noise of the little man's firing, for which Rand was very grateful.

Amy stood for a moment, looking at the body, and then she turned to face Rand. "I'd like a drink," she said.

"Anything you want," Rand answered as he dragged the body to the edge and rolled it off, turning back when he heard it hit bottom.

"Jack, if you got it…" she said.

"I didn't know you drank."

"I don't, but Jack Daniels sounds good right now." She sat and put the .380 in her lap. Rand hurried over to help Jim up. He was pretty banged up, bleeding from his mouth and above his left eye.

The rancher cleaned and bandaged the wounds, not speaking except to instruct the heavy set man when to turn and how to take care of himself. He was still angry that Jim had been no help during the firefight. The portly rancher was properly abashed and wisely said nothing. Rand doused the lights and trudged below, carrying Primero to the field and clearing the other bodies from the passageway. He would worry about any searchers in the morning. To his thinking, whoever he killed was expendable, even Primero.

Done with the bodywork, Rand washed himself and dressed his own wound until Amy stepped in to minister to him. It took a half hour to get cleaned up. She brought him food and water cheerfully. The rancher wondered if she remembered shooting Primero. As he sat to eat, Amy pulled a camp cot close and began to share what else she found among the goods that Jim had stored in the stronghold.

She was like a little girl for the moment, talking with a clarity Rand had not heard in years. The southern drawl was back and quite pronounced, and she used phrases like "I swan to goodness" and "not so much as a fare thee well." He wondered how old she was in her head.

Jim curled up in a corner and slept, and Amy opened her pockets to reveal what she found. She produced a wind-up survival all band radio that she thought was a jack in the box. It was a find. Rand showed her how to work it and was about to settle into a rest when the radio poured out a static laden news report, something about border skirmishes in Texas and California. While it was hard to decipher what little came through, the rancher heard about the drug cartels firing on border agents and about the feds sending in agents and the National Guard from neighboring states to man the border.

Rand's first thought was "misdirection." He was too tired to think about it, but what Primero said repeated and repeated in his memory, superimposing itself over, "There's too many, Shane. Too many." As he dropped off to sleep, the rancher sensed the wind change and come in from the west. Intermittent sounds of machinery like the sounds of highway making wafted up and bounced off the butte.

Rand slept. Amy sat on a camp cot near him and watched all night.

Chapter 6

If you can't see tomorrow from up here, you're not lookin'

Amy awakened her nephew before dawn. There was movement far up the cattle trail. A large stake bed truck, too big for the trail, not big enough to roll over the dunes without difficulty. Rand woke Jim and told him to put enough provisions together to last for several days, plus a desert camo tarp and the weapons. He went into the adobe and led Beamer out by enticing him with hay. He wrapped a shirt over the draft's head and led him down the passageway to the field below, then he slapped the horse on the rump, and the draft made his way east over the rock field.

The rancher hurried back up the passageway into the cliff dwelling and brought Jim and Amy to the chimney where Jim had rigged the rope in days past. "We have to get out of here, and this is the only way."

Jim felt he was in no shape to make the climb, but Amy embarrassed him into it by saying, "let's get started." Rand bent a double bowline in the middle of the rope and demonstrated how she was to sit in it when he signaled, and then he shinnied up the forty feet to the top and called down for her to get into the seat. It took five minutes of careful lifting to get her to the top with the portly neighbor helping to guide her along the channel.

When Amy stepped out of the seat, she stood aside as Rand let the rope back down.

"Jim. Tie the bundle to the end of the rope, then get into the seat. You're gonna have to help me 'cause I can't lift you all alone, okay?" he called down the shaft and got no response. Amy called into the shaft "Don't make me come down there and get you." A feeble "Yes, ma'am," was all that came back.

When Rand felt the tug on the rope, he lifted Jim through the chimney. It took twice as long as Amy's trip, and when the heavyset man had completed the trip he swore to lose weight. The comment was so natural and meaningless vis a vis the situation, Rand and Amy laughed. The tension was broken. Jim felt he could talk now. They jointly hoisted the provisions and weapons and coiled the rope neatly near the entrance to the shaft.

"We have to obscure the shaft so they won't know we're up here. Cover it with the tarp. We should get it done before sunup," Rand ordered, and Jim obeyed immediately while Rand crept to the edge of the butte and looked over the landscape below.

The truck had found the rock field, and a large crew of men in fatigues worked diligently to retrieve, bag, and stack the bodies aboard. The rancher was surprised to see how quickly and how precisely the team worked. At dawn when they finished with the bodies, a dozen men lifted and carried beach burned out SUVs to separate spots between dunes and covered them with sand and brush, perfectly matching the surrounding landscape.

Rand admired the work. It was well and professionally done. He automatically counted the detail and judged it at platoon strength. He wondered if this party would join the search for him, Amy, and Jim, but once the bodies had been bagged and tagged, the truck and men backed up the trail, losing a body every now and then, which was quickly retrieved. After thirty minutes, they were gone.

The sun rose over a low fog that hugged the desert floor, common in this season. Rand found a convenient place, a depression near the center of the crest of the butte adjoining the shaft into the niche below and set up a shelter using the camo tarp. He worked to make the site comfortable for Amy, and she settled in for her stay.

"Have we been up here before?" she asked. Amy had slipped back into the refuge of her forgetfulness.

"No," Rand answered. "We've never been up here."

Jim joined them from the edge. "Wanted to apologize for lettin' you down last night. It's just that.... well, I never shot anybody before..."

Rand stopped him. "Why didn't you say something?"

"I actually thought I could do it...it's just that when it came right down to it.... I couldn't." He paused. "It's different from a deer."

"Yeah...real different." Rand crept to the western edge with the field glasses. He was curious about the machinery he'd heard last night. He intended to concentrate on the far western canyons, but something about a mile due west caught his eye. He shifted his view to see twelve men in desert camouflage walking north along the wide wash where he'd seen the machinery during the firefight.

Rand tightened his focus to more closely examine the squad. Each man carried a desert camo ghillie suit, half carried spotter cases, half carried cases Rand knew to be HK 50 cases. A quarter mile behind the squad, two rear guard men followed as if on a Sunday stroll.

It puzzled the rancher that snipers walked so casually, like they were going to a practice range. That they had a rear guard made less sense. He followed their progress for a mile until they split into six teams and spread out over high points near a specific canyon. Two teams settled onto brushy dunes on the flats. Rand realized they were placed to cover the mouth of the canyon. In a few minutes, the two teams were undercover.

Rand made a mental note as to their positions. They were too far away to hit from the top of the butte, but he needed to know where they were. The other four teams scaled the nose walls of the canyon and crawling over the edges to set up from a high point, one team on the outer edge, covering the entrance, and the other two teams farther back, able to cover from the middle of the canyon all the way to the back. They, too, got under cover immediately, disappearing into the low hanging fog.

It occurred to him that the sniper teams were within striking distance of each other and that their focus was not away from the canyon, but toward it. These were not defensive positions. They were more like prison camp installations. He swung his view in to get a closer look at the canyon, which was still filled with the morning fog.

Behind him, the sun sneaked over the horizon, half revealed between the land and an overcast sky. The storm from last night was a longer drawn out affair than usual. Normally such storms came up suddenly, dropped huge amounts of rain, and then fled as quickly as they came, but the cloudy conditions remained telling the rancher that another downpour was on its way.

Rand pushed the zoom in to take a long careful look at what little the fog left to see. Faint noise of machinery disturbed the desert quiet, but the rancher saw nothing but an occasional swirl of moist air above where the machines worked. He knew the area well.

The canyon floor dropped off from the desert flats into a deep depression, it ran back more than three hundred yards, and it had very steep sides. The tops resembled mesas like the rest of the hills and had a crust of hard rock caps that were five to six feet thick. The caps were nearly white and little or no vegetation grew within fifteen yards of the edges.

The canyon itself was a forbidding place. The rancher's herds sometimes took shelter from storms, both dust and rain, in the deeper recesses, but in heavy downpours, the depression could fill as much as twenty feet deep. Flash floods could take out an entire herd in a few minutes. For reasons only animals know, this was the exact spot they sought.

Rand had learned through bad experience that this was the first place to look when the storms approached. This year, not a good one for the cattle business, he sold off the herd early and prepared to sit out the next season to wait for feed to go down and beef to come up. It was a wise move as it turned out.

The south wind turned cold as the clouds thickened and boiled north. Not yet seven o'clock, the rancher watched as the breeze scuttled the fog from the flats and revealed the positions of the embedded snipers. From his vantage point, Rand detected each position clearly and saw some movement in the canyon, but he couldn't see much. The sound of the machinery diminished in the wind.

Jim, who had taken a position on the southern rim of the butte, grunted. Rand glanced over and saw the heavyset man motion that he should take a look. The rancher crossed the butte and sat cross-legged next to his neighbor.

It was not unexpected. A squad of armed men entered the rock field via the cattle trail and made their way directly toward the entrance to the stronghold. Jim readied his rifle, but Rand stopped him.

"Save it. We should be okay," was all he said, and he went to the top of the chimney to listen. Rand counted the time it would take to mount to the stronghold and bent down to listen to what they might say. Amy sat and watched, not making a sound.

Below, the squad made it to the niche. Rand could hear their discussions; the talk was not in a language he understood, but it was clear that the team intended to use the niche as a staging area for themselves. Not good.

Again, Jim grunted and motioned Rand over to his lookout. He pointed toward the southeast, indicating another squad scouring the desert near the arroyo. The rancher guessed that they would find the three bodies of the flankers he'd killed. He also surmised that they were looking for him and Amy, and maybe Jim, but he wasn't worried. They could only be seen from the air.

"Where's your ATV?" he asked Jim who pointed southwest.

It started to rain the first little droplets, and the two joined Amy, spreading the tarp over their heads. Thunder broke to the southeast, and Jim got a frightened look on his face. Rand laughed, "Hell, Jim, we don't need to worry about gettin' lightnin' struck. They're probably gonna shoot us anyway." Amy laughed out loud at that.

The rancher gathered up the provisions and moved the other two toward a spot that was lower. He spread out the tarp and anchored it with rocks. They huddled down inside and waited, watching the opening in the chimney

The storm became more violent with high winds, not unexpected in this exposure, and with heavy rain, which puddled beneath their feet.

Amy seemed to be doing all right, not that anyone could tell. She sat, much as she did in the house, lost in thought, humming a hymn every once in a while. The storm did not seem to bother her in the least. Rand slept fitfully, and Jim stewed quietly, watching the opening, and searching the horizon every few minutes.

The morning passed, but the rain continued to fall sporadically. Rand spent the time considering what to do next. He believed the activity in the canyon was the key to unlock the reasons for the whole attack. What little he'd heard on Amy's jack in the box radio led him to think that the border events in Texas and California were diversionary.

"Too Many, Shane, too many," Brandon deWilde's voice was right. There were too many bad guys down there for this to be anything small. The other attacks, nobody showing up here, obscuring due to bad weather, movement under cover of night all came together in his mind. What Misael and Primero had to say piqued his instincts, long dormant as they were. And whatever the big deal was, it was right here.

Jeeze, he thought. Where were the good guys?

Rand dozed again, letting the thoughts float around in his head. Long range recon, need to know basis, air assault, search and destroy were phrases he'd not countenanced for decades; but now, they cascaded back.

The rancher was exhausted. Jim's dithering about did nothing to help him rest. Neither did the memory of his wife and son's death. He'd not had time to think about their last minutes. Had they awakened, or had they been simply dispatched with a couple of quick shots? Had they known terror?

Carol had said that the last words she wanted hear on earth was that Rand loved her, and that was so. She always went to bed earlier than he did because his snoring would not let her sleep. She would check on their twelve year old then she would let her husband doze on the couch. It was an old and comfortable habit.

They were both on the second go round in marriage, but it worked, mainly because of who she was.

The boy would go to bed early, never having to be coaxed. When he was tired, he went to bed: a good kid, a funny kid, and with a droll sense of humor. Once when the brakes went out on a mountain road, after Rand got the truck stopped by coasting onto a rollout, the boy calmly said, "Dad, this 'ole living on the edge has got to end." That was four years ago. Funny how a message from God can come out of the mouth of an eight-year-old.

Yeah, he thought. It's got to end. And end it did, a big change for Rand. Ranch work was hard, but it was successful, due mainly to Carol's encouragement and the responsibility of a son. Having a kid at fifty-eight is either very optimistic or very stupid. The rancher felt he was on the point of finding out which in the last couple of weeks.

The rancher made a point of "finishing his business" with his family. They never left anything unsaid. He had learned that in combat. Because one never knew if his buddies would live through a mission, one always finished the personal business. It was easier to do that than to carry around recrimination. The habit carried into later life, and it worked.

Rand had no regrets about Carol or Chuck other than what the future could have held for them. He did regret that he'd not paid more attention to the signs that something was ready to happen. If Jim got it, why didn't he?

Amy had come to live with them three years ago when she ran out of money to stay in the retirement home. Her own kin would not take her in, and typical of Carol who never met a lost dog she wouldn't take in, she insisted they take in the missionary's widow. It was difficult at first, but Carol made a way.

The rain eased, and Rand left the cover to have a look around. He checked below and saw the search team heading back toward the butte from the east. He heard the voices of the men in the niche and felt trapped. Amy sat under the shelter staring blankly at him. Jim fretted. His portly neighbor had "victim" written all over him. Rand's aunt had "need" written all over her.

The rancher was suddenly angry, as angry as he'd ever been. Here he was, trapped with enemies surrounding him from every side but above, his only two allies, one who had no awareness of the situation, and another who was acutely aware but was impotent to do anything to help.

His assessment of the situation was pretty bad. Rand looked back over the side of the butte and spotted a four-man team following the western wash down the flats toward the canyon. They carried heavy packs, but they moved quickly. The rancher knew the look. They were demolition guys, and, in the wash, they were close enough to take out with the .50 calibers, but he was not set up.

He mentioned the passing to Jim who wanted to try the shots, but Rand cautioned him that any fire would alert the squads below them. The heavy set man was more than anxious to redeem himself in his neighbor's eyes, but he was also smart enough to realize the risks.

He shook his head still angry, and now he was even more confused than ever. Rand didn't know what these people were doing, but he made up his mind that whatever it was that they had planned, he was going to make it doing it difficult.

The focus of their operation had shifted to the canyon. The men below him in the cliff dwelling were sentries of one kind or another. The men who approached from the east were raiders. The snipers were close support for the canyon, but the demolition guys and the machinery operators were still a mystery.

The weather lightened up by noon. The cloud cover remained and kept the heat down. Rand spent the afternoon cleaning the AK and loading up magazines while Jim retrieved the .50 from its case and being educated on a fire and move strategy if things went to hell in a hand basket. After the rancher located a tie-off on the northern face of the butte, they rested between moments of checking the movements of the men on the flats.

Amy insisted on redressing their wounds. For some reason, she awakened from a short nap and was a young Texas girl again, bright and alert, attentive to her duties. She opened food packets and made sure the men were fed.

Late in the day, Jim noticed several men from the search squad to the north of the butte. He guessed it was a scouting party because the group wandered as far as a mile north and a mile or so west, keeping away from the mouth of the canyon. It was as if a line had been drawn 500 yards from the opening because when they approached the imaginary demarcation, the men abruptly turned back as one man and cut back directly for the butte, coming in on its west side.

Rand watched and counted four, adding it to the number he believed to be in the strong hold, he guessed the total to be eighteen, too many to fight with what he had. It was possible that Jim could get a bunch of them if they decided to leave via the passageway. It was open at the top, and, by leaning over the southern edge of the butte, the heavyset man could pick them off. He would have a maximum of ten or fifteen seconds before they could return fire due to the element of surprise, but then, his position would have been revealed.

The rancher observed another thing that puzzled him. The four man team he had seen earlier on the wash worked along the ridge that surrounded the canyon, planting charges every twenty or thirty yards. He knew from experience that the explosives would sever a line that would collapse sending thousands of tons of soil into the floor of the canyon. He wondered why all the digging only to cover it up…with explosives.

One thing was sure. Sitting on top of a butte in the middle of nowhere was not going to satisfy his curiosity, nor would sitting there ameliorate his present situation.

Oddly, he thought, the person who was doing best up here was Amy, but the exposure, long term, would eventually weaken her. Added to that, Jim's dithering was still getting to him.

<u>Chapter Seven</u>

There's a Reason Curiosity Killed the Cat

When it was nearly dark, the sun down for twenty minutes, Rand put together his weaponry, the AK, the Sig, his assault knife, and enough ammo to last for a good long firefight. Using surgical tape from the first aid kit, he taped three magazines together in staggered rows so he wouldn't have to fumble for reloads. The rancher then blacked up his face and hands with charcoal and petroleum jelly. He was ready.

As soon as the darkness was complete, artificial lights glimmered to life in the canyon. The machinery's awakening was attested to by sounds coming from the canyon.

It was time to go.

Rand bent over and kissed Amy on the forehead. She glanced up briefly and the wisp of a smile crossed her lips. "Be careful, and come back to get me when you can." He nodded and went to the northern side of the butte crest. He checked the tie off and hurled the balance of the rope as far out as its weight would carry.

Jim stood by and helped Rand get his battle gear on. "When the rope goes slack, look and see if I'm down, then pull it up and coil it. Then, I want you to cover the guys in the dwelling. If they leave in a hurry, get as many as you can. If they stroll out, leave 'em alone. It's more important that you both stay hidden.

Remember what I said about the .50?" Jim nodded. "That's the big deal. Cover me."

Jim wanted to say something, but Rand wouldn't let him. "We were lucky once. That's all we get." He laced the rope around himself as best he could remember how and dropped over the edge.

Amy murmured, "No weapon formed against thee shall prosper. Ye shall run and not be weary, walk and not faint."

Rand was concerned that the snipers around the canyon would have IR equipment and would be able to spot him. He hoped that the heat of the granite would obscure him long enough for him to get to the rock field below. The snipers closest were facing the canyon so they might not become aware of him. He was still out of range, unless they were very, very good, and from what he saw when they came down the wash, they weren't.

The snipers on the rim at the mouth of the canyon were the ones to worry about. They were covering the two in the flats and the opening to the canyon. They, too, were out of range, but they were high enough and far enough out of the work lights, that they would be able to spot him…if they looked.

The vision of the two teams at the far end was "brighted" out due to the work lights, so Rand dispensed the risk they posed.

The rancher worked his way down; slowly rappelling in small increments to avoid making noise that might draw attention, it took every second of a full ten minutes to reach the rock field. It felt good to move. He trotted due north, wanting to be off the rock field and out of a no-cover zone as quickly as possible, and he was relieved when he sensed the end of the boulders and the beginning of the desert sand.

Rand paused for a moment to take on water and cast a glance back toward the butte. A hint of light from the canyon work lights played on it, making it look bigger than it was. He felt good for the first time since the ranch was attacked. Yesterday was a bitch, but now he was rested.

The rancher launched into his scouter's pace, fifty walking, fifty jogging, following the meandering terrain of dunes and flats. In ten minutes, he slowed, turned west, and mounted the nearest dune, avoiding the prickly pear. He was positioned dead center of the mouth of the canton, maybe five hundred yards east of the snipers' tangent. He held a crouch and studied what he saw.

The glare of the lights was quite pronounced, the actual instruments poised ten feet below the rim, spaced forty feet along each side until they met at the back of the canyon. The view to where the machines worked was not good, but he could see dust rise in short bursts, and he could hear the straining of the enormous engines as they plied the earth.

Rand backtracked down the dune and turned north again. He did a mile in ten minutes and turned west until he came to the wide outflow of the wash. It was a good bet that the flats snipers had taken positions on the east side, but he was far enough away that they would not be able to hear him. He descended the

edge and crossed the wash. When he mounted the
low rise on the other side, the rancher slanted right
and made for the second, shallower canyon to the
north.

Rand knew this place well. It was a great place to
bring down antelope and javelina. It was not as long
as the subject canyon, running just half as far west,
and its walls were not as steep.

When he arrived at the very backside, Rand rested for
a few minutes, surprised at his relaxed state. The
rancher climbed the southern slope and ditched his
pack a few feet short of the rim. He slung the rifle
under his arm and poked his head above the rim.

Seventy yards to his left he saw the north canyon
mouth sniper team lying prone, but up on their
elbows smoking cigarettes. To his right, at maybe a
hundred yards, he could make out the end canyon
team. They were asleep.

The cap of the mesa, or what they called a mesa, was
sedimentary rock, one to two feet thick, sparsely
populated with small scrags of woody shrubs, one
thin stalk that became spare green leaves. Not much
cover and hard, unforgiving ground to cross if he
wanted to attack.

The rancher checked the cove at the end of the
canyon. A small berm stood back about twenty feet
from the rim that could provide cover. He needed to
see inside the canyon proper, so he picked up his
pack and trekked along below the rim until he came
to a place where he could clamber over the thick
bluff onto the upper flats. He was fifty yards from the

sleeping snipers, a hundred and fifty from the smokers.

Rand trotted lightly due west and circled around to come up on the west side of the berm. From this point, he saw all four of the sniper teams on the rim. The southern teams were just as useless as the northern teams, one team playing cards, the other chatting. He lied on his belly and crept, rifle in hand, to a recon position and looked into the canyon.

The rancher had a good vantage point from which to see all but the area at the foot of the bluff nearest him. The lights, which rimmed the canyon, were daylight bright xenon units, eight per side and two immediately before him on the back rim of the canyon. They appeared to have been set by the crane rig that sat at the halfway point of the canyon trough. They were expensive lights: two rows of four, one above another like those in stadia. Their stanchions had been pounded into the slope by a pile driver extension that lay next to the flatbed sitting ahead of the crane. A generator on the flatbed ran full bore and powered the lights and other equipment.

On the opposite side of the flatbed sat a number of steel half cylinders perhaps six foot in diameter and eight feet long with interlocking flanges that ran along all sides. They looked very well constructed, and the metal appeared to be at least an inch thick. The rancher could tell from the indentations in the dirt that six sections were already assembled with six left to go.

Rand let his view trail down the slope to a series of wires that traced along within five or six feet above the bases of the stanchions. Every twenty feet, the wires disappeared into the soil. He judged this was where the explosives were set.

Directly in front of Rand, a large, new front loader worked around a small area forty yards away in the deepest depression of the canyon. He counted the number of men working. The crane operator, and likely the driver, was one. The operator of the front loader made two. Two men worked by the loose half cylinders as tie-ups, and, he suspected, four worked as cylinder assemblers. That made eight altogether.

Beyond the generator on the flatbed was a cargo box with breakaway latches on the tops and sides. It looked like it was fifty feet long by ten. It bore no markings whatever.

The crew below worked quickly, assembling two sections in less than thirty minutes. When two pieces were joined, the front loader scooped dirt in around it and compacted the soil until it was within six inches of the top of the last assemblage. As the loader worked, the crane swung around to pick up another steel section and swinging it in for placement in minutes.

It was a well-practiced team, something Rand had seen before. While he was not sure what this was, he had a good idea, and he suspected the answer was hidden in the cargo box.

The rancher looked back toward the nearest sniper and found they were not as stupid or ignorant as he had originally thought. Here in better light, he saw something very familiar behind their positions. Each team on the rim was backed up by two claymore mines. Good protection. He couldn't see trip wires, but he was sure they were there. He hoped it made them overconfident, a failing he'd seen in their compatriots.

Ego's a killer, he thought and crawled back down the hill to rest and hydrate.

An hour passed, and the rancher crawled back to the top of the little hill for another look at the happenings in the canyon.

The iron tube was complete, and the soil was within six inches of the top. The workers near the flatbed wrestled with what appeared to be a large tan fiberglass cap for the cylindrical structure. It was light enough for three men to move, but its bulk proved unmanageable until it was put into crane sling straps and hoisted to a point near the cylinder.

The crane rested open side up allowing Rand to see the interior. It was fitted with an electronic device that looked more like an old stereo tuner hooked up to metal tape which spiraled from the topmost point of the cone all the way down to where the cap would join the now buried cylinder. One thick cable dangled from the electronics unit as if waiting to be plugged into something. The chassis of the electronic unit contained indicator lights that flashed in a familiar "ready" mode. On two inner sides, long pigtails of what looked like C-4 ropes ran from the peak to the flat flange of the cone.

Rand returned his focus to the large container where the flatbed crew unclipped large latches along the upper edges of the box. The crane swung over and carefully lifted the top away and set it beside the flatbed, leaning it against the trailer and letting it settle to the ground before releasing it. Meanwhile the crew unlatched the very back end of the box and let it hinge down to meet the body of the trailer, giving him a clear view of what sat inside the box.

The rancher swore a blue streak under his breath. Surprise is one thing, but dread is quite another. He'd seen some bad things in his life, but this was one of the worst.

As the crew dropped the last sides of the box, its content came into view. The glare of the lights was as bright as a hospital surgery. The illumination revealed a rectangular framework of steel I-bars, which cradled a two and a half foot diameter thirty-foot long missile body. The framework was fitted with lifting shackles to which the crane cable was quickly attached.

The lifting process was tedious and very slow. The crane strained as it tilted the frame and its cargo to vertical. Rand deemed it to be a single stage solid fuel booster minus its warhead. When the rig became totally vertical, he could see that the engine nozzle sat on a steel web platform some six feet from the lower end of the frame. At six foot intervals were guidance rails mounted on rings that girded the missile body.

This baby was ready to fire the instant it mounted inside the cylinder. The rancher had to admire the technique. He hoped that Jim would be able to see this, but doubted it was possible from this angle.

The crane groaned as it brought the frame to height and armed over to set it into the cylinder. The crews watched intently, as did the snipers, as the frame was eased into its cocoon. The frame slid perfectly into place, and two crewmen unshackled it and waved away the cable. Rand detected a tension he had not as yet witnessed.

The crane armed back to its position over the flatbed and rested over a smaller box. Two men unlatched the cover of the box and attached slings to the equipment inside. Again, the crane strained on lifting the piece. The reach was not as high this time, but it was clear that the payload was heavy. The attachment crew stood immediately away from the white thing that resembled a giant eggcup. It lifted slowly, more deliberately, and was gingerly swung toward the silo.

Rand had seen enough. His first choice was to fire into the missile, but he knew that solid fuel needed extremely high temperature to ignite, so that was not an option. The rancher had to get away, get help, and he was about to shed everything but the AK and the Sig when movement below attracted his attention.

Two men working at the top of the cylinder adjusted the framework and guided the egg shaped module onto the upper end of the missile body. In a remarkably short time, they seated the module and ran snap bolts home. They stood for a moment to admire their work and signaled for the crane to extend more cable to be attached to the fiberglass cone.

The cone lifted abruptly to a point just above their heads. One steadied the cone, and the other stretched the hanging cable into the cylinder. The cable man bent over the edge of the cylinder and attached the cable to a slot on the egg shaped module. He then signaled the crane operator to lower the cone.

The cone settled snugly onto the cylinder, and the four men near it shoveled earth loosely over the top until it was covered with several inches of sand while the crane operator set the arm into its travel cradle, ready to leave. Then, the crew marched smartly down toward the flatbed where a tall man waited, waving money above his head.

Something is not right, Rand thought to himself. He noticed that the sniper teams were suddenly on point. The work crews lined up along the side of the flatbed, chattering happily. The tall man looked familiar, but standing in the half-light, the rancher could not truly distinguish the features.

In seconds, the snipers on the rim opened fire, killing every last man on the work crew, including the crane operator in less than fifteen seconds. The tall man looked over the bodies and waved the sniper teams away. The four teams on the rim of the canyon dropped everything but the weaponry and headed east.

In the calm, the rancher heard two vehicles below leave, and he assumed they were going back up the wash. Still, something was not right. Why would they leave all those bodies lying out when they had been so careful to recover and bury all the other bodies?

Uh-oh, he thought. The explosives that had been planted earlier were still there. He picked up his bag, turned and ran west as hard as he could. It was too late. The characteristic whump-whump-whump sound of sequential charges pumped against the pre-dawn air, knocking him to the ground. The work lights snuffed out, and Rand heard earth collapse into the canyon.

He tried to get up, but the wind was knocked out of him. Rand rolled over to catch his breath and saw Venus go obscure in the dust cloud from the explosives. It was the last thing he remembered before everything went black.

Chapter Eight

Escape is Just Another Word for Nothin' Left to Lose

Cold. Dark. Rand came to. His wrists and ankles were bound with plastic snap ties, and he was buck naked, lying on his side on a wood floor that moved and bounced around like a van truck barreling along a desert road that, in fact, was true. He wasn't gagged. Not that it made any difference, the van felt old, and it was noisy.

As the rancher grew accustomed to the light, or lack of same, he could see sunlight coming through little empty rivet holes on the left side of the box. He was headed south and wished he'd awakened earlier so he'd know how far they traveled. The van bounced again and jolted him bodily a foot into the air, and when he hit the floor, he felt the rugged planking dig into his flesh.

Rand had no idea how he'd gotten here. He remembered the explosions and the impact, but after that, nothing.

The limited light, the coolness of the van box told him that it was still early in the day, and that was a good thing. The sound of the truck motor labored, never getting to third gear. Another good thing. The driver was pressing for some reason; otherwise, the pace would have been less pushed. Rand wondered how many were in the cab.

His eyes adjusted to what light there was and saw that the front of the van box was stacked to the top with filled body bags, two deep that occupied the front half. No wonder it smelled so bad in here.

Rand rolled left to find the metal wall of the van, picking up slivers along the way, but he needed to stabilize from the jolts of the truck moving along what must have been a road…of sorts. His hands and feet were cold from lack of circulation. They were barely moveable. He latched onto a packing rail by slipping one hand under and one over the wooden slat.

They could have left me my shorts, he thought. The truck continued for another twenty minutes, then it ground to a stop. Rand got ready by releasing his hold on the rail and putting his hands up in front of his face. He heard some discussion in Spanish, picking up a few words, but unable to make any sense of them. Then, he heard the hasps on the roll-up door throw.

The light streamed in, and the rancher got his first look at his captors. The two men looked small from his vantage point above them. He thought about making a move on them, but considering his present state of undress, it seemed better to not. They were laughing at him. It was not friendly mirth.

The huskier of the two climbed into the van box, grabbed his wrist restraints, and hauled Rand to his feet. He pulled the rancher forward and kicked him out of the van. He landed hard and fell to the rocky roadbed, unable to stand. The two laughed again, and

Rand decided to play weak, which was not a stretch. He was exhausted, thirsty, and hungry, in that order.

The Latin's looked bigger from this angle, but surprisingly, they made no move to beat on him. One sat on the edge of the truck bed, and the other paced back and forth on the shady side of the van.

Rand sat up and looked around. He had no idea where they were. He guessed they were south of the border by a good distance. The landscape was like that of the ranch, and from the look of it, the road was a major route used by the drogeros and illegals. He rested his elbows on his knees and his forehead on his hands. Using this pose, he could cover where he was looking.

The rancher turned his body so he could face west. Pretending to wipe his eyes, he got a good look at the tracks made by the tires of the van, noting that one of the rear tires was nearly bald, and the opposite was almost new. He glanced left and was able to assess the smaller of his captors.

The man wore the same quasi-uniform as those in the first raid. Both men were covered in dust with sweat-drenched shirts. Curiously, neither was armed. The pacer was in charge, but not by much, and no one spoke after bringing him out of the van.

They sat for thirty minutes, and then an SUV emerged from the south in a cloud of dust. It ran hard until it was within fifty yards, then it skidded to a stop. The driver's door opened, and a large man exited, striding purposefully toward the sitting rancher.

Rand recognized the tall man as the one he'd nicknamed Guapo, and instantly knew that the man who had lured the work crews in the canyon to their demise was the same guy. The tall man shaded his eyes against the morning sun and stooped to look directly into Rand's face.

"My research on you was inadequate, I must admit," Guapo said in flawless English.

Rand made no answer, but looked directly into the man's eyes. This guy was no Latino. His manner was aristocratic, not quite arrogant, but close enough. Middle eastern, he guessed. It fit. Better clothes, expensive, good boots.

Guapo stood. "How many are you?" Guapo asked.

"Just me," Rand answered.

"Not buying it, old man," his captor replied. "How many?"

"Just me."

Guapo launched a quick soccer style kick to the rancher's head, sending him to his side. "No one is that good…. you're saying that you alone killed that many of my people?" He launched another kick to the rancher's chest. "Do you take me for stupid?" then angrily,
"How many, kafir?"

"Nobody else. I got lucky."

"You are dealing with an educated scholar, old man. MIT. I have lived in this country fifteen years. You are too old to have done this. There have to be others."

"No one." Rand wished he had a weapon, anything.

"What about the old woman?"

"She died, first night."

"What about this Broderick fellow?"

"Never saw him."

Guapo paced away. "No matter then." He called out to the pacing Latino in perfect Spanish, "Ydisrio, desea matarlo?" (Would you like to kill him?)

The slender Latino nodded that he did.

To Rand he said, "You killed his brother, Misael. I think you knew him."

"Used to work for me."

"Yes. He said you were always fair, but he was ready to kill you for the cause…"

"What cause?"

"Aztlan. That's how we got them to help us." Guapo was dying to tell someone. "It was a magnificent alliance."

"Why tell me?" the rancher asked, showing little interest.

"Because I want at least one of you stupid Americans to know in advance what is going to happen to your apostate country. I want someone to hear it, to dread it, to wait for it." He paced about like a headmaster in front of the class dunce.

Guapo drew himself up to full height. "I made an arrangement with the drug cartels, the Aztlaneros to make skirmishes in Texas, New Mexico, and California while I brought the missile in. It is brilliant, don't you think?" He kicked Rand in the leg as he passed. "Simple, but brilliant. Then, I trained these people using what I learned with your military."

Rand got the idea. "For what?"

"For what? Are all Americans so stupid? I invented the idea of firing an EMP device from inside your homeland where there is no defense. Your military expects it to come from the oceans, not from inside. Seven minutes, and your electronics are destroyed over a two thousand mile radius."

"When?" Rand croaked, his throat dry.

"Soon. We are ready to fight a small country, but we are not ready to fight the U.S. We will let you destroy yourselves. The device will give us time."

"You realize we will counterattack."

"We are prepared for it, but you will be too late. The Mahdi will return, and then, no one can stop us."

"Why tell me?"

Guapo leaned in close to Rand's ear. "I want you to see it, to know what it is when it happens."

The tall man looked toward the two Latinos, holding his hand up to brush them away. "You think I'm going to let Ysidrio kill you? No, my friend. I have decided to let you live so you can see this happen.... if you make it back." He pulled his pistol from his scabbard and fired twice, killing both Ysidrio and his compatriot. Guapo returned his focus to the rancher.

"Even if you do make it back, there's no one there to help you. We killed them all, or bought them. Border agents, law enforcement, everybody.... you are alone." The tall man laughed and walked casually to his SUV. "Besides, nobody would believe you in time." He laughed again, started the vehicle and maneuvered alongside the van where he fired twice into the fuel tanks of the van, which burst into flame instantly.

Guapo drove south and disappeared in the ensuing cloud of dust.

Rand was on his feet and hopping toward the bodies of the Latinos as quickly as he could. Burning fuel leaked into puddles around the bodies setting them ablaze. The rancher hauled Ysidrio's body away from the burning fuel and rolled it as best he could to extinguish the flames. He searched the body for something with which to cut his shackles and found a knife in the man's front pocket.

The rancher opened then jammed the knife into the ground to make a ready cutting surface. The tool was very sharp and sliced away one wrist shackle, freeing his left hand. Not stopping to cut away the snap tie on his right wrist, he pulled the knife from the soil and used it to free his feet.

Able to move, Rand trotted to see if the cab of the truck could be entered, but the fire licked it on all sides. He ran back to the box. Its front was fully engulfed, but the flames had not yet reached the opening. He vaulted inside and hurried to the body bags. Smoke emanated from the front of the box and filled the inside in seconds.

He picked the biggest bulk, towed it to the back, and rolled it off the rim. Rand jumped off the back of the van and hauled the bag away from the fire. He unzipped the bag and tore the edges away from the body inside. He was in luck.

The body inside was of a man about his size and stiff as a board. He rolled the body out and uncovered it. The rancher pulled the boots off the body first, then the pants and shirt. It all bore the stench of death, but he was beyond caring. His attention was distracted by the sounds of ammo exploding in the cab of the van. There was no time to lose. He grabbed the knife he had retrieved from Ysidrio's body, as well as the clothing, and sprinted north on the road till he came to a dune where he took cover.

The rancher judged it was about seven or seven-thirty, but he had no idea where he was. He assessed his situation while he shook out the clothing and ran mesquite foliage inside the arms and legs of the camo. He scanned north to see any familiar landmark. There was none.

Rand needed water for right now and for later if he were to take on a forced march back to the ranch. The rounds had stopped cooking off from the fire. It didn't mean it was safe to go back because another set could start at any time, but he decided to chance it to see if there was anything to scavenge.

He started back. The boots were a little big for his feet. At the moment, it didn't matter, but it would in a few hours.

The fire stunk from burned flesh. The van was little more than a bare chassis that served as a funeral pyre. The only recognizable bodies were those of Ysidrio and the one Rand had pulled from the body bag. Neither had any water on them. Ysidrio's weapon lay between his body and the burning chassis. The nylon stock was melted. Rand wondered if the action still served.

Using the knife, the rancher dragged it away from the heat and set it in the shade to cool. He sat down to rest and to examine himself for damage. Aside from the splinters in his backside, Rand was pretty much intact. His wrists and ankles were sore from the restraints, but everything else worked.

Rand stood, ready to move north. He would follow the road whence he had come. The rains of yesterday would have puddled somewhere, and he would find the puddle. He had to leave this place. The consciousness of the missile was all the encouragement he needed. The rifle was cool enough to pick up. He racked back the ejector. It was a little sticky, but it might work if necessary. He dared not rack off a shot because he had just one magazine.

He headed out.

In two hours, the rancher judged he'd covered seven or eight miles. He'd not counted more than the first few hundred yards, after that it was a judgment call. He knew he was headed north. From the litter along the road, he could tell he was on a major smuggling route, but the fact that he saw not one other human being nagged at him. Funny how regular people sense when something heavy is about to happen, and for sure, this was one of those times.

The desert was silent. Birds did not call. He saw no rabbits or snakes. It was as if everything had gone to ground. It was just as well. Rand was in no mood to warn anybody away, nor was he in a mood to have to fight it out with a drogero team, and needed no interruption.

The rancher mused over whether Guapo had been truthful when he made the statements about killing off Border Patrol and law enforcement. If not, the rancher would find help after he crossed the border. He hoped Guapo was as big a liar as he was a killer, but he didn't count on it.

He guessed he was still south of the border that meant the Federales could show up anytime. That would not be good, considering the burned van, the bodies, and his current state of armament. Rand's former dealings with Mexican authorities over stray horses involved bribes, lots of explanation. If they were bad about a few horses, forty or so bodies and a burnt out van would be a nightmare, but normally the Federales kept away from the smuggling routes unless there was big money involved. Why take the risk?

He spotted a small, deep arroyo off to his left that showed dark sand in the shadows. The rancher knew water would be close to the surface, so he hopped down to the bottom, knelt and began to scoop sand out until he felt the dampness turn to mud, then the mud to water. He let the water still a moment, and then he put a cupped hand in to scoop out a drink.

As Rand drank his fill, spitting out sand, he thought about Jim and Amy, hoping they were still alive. He further hoped they had stayed put and had not ventured out to the canyon to search for him. Jim was probably scared enough to stay away from any fighting. Amy, for sure, wouldn't. He finished the thought and started to crawl out of the arroyo when he heard the very familiar chopping sound of a helicopter, flying at low altitude, coming north, following the road he'd just left.

The rancher was on the point of scrambling onto the road to signal the aircraft when something in his head made him pause. He let himself slide back down into the gulley until he was at eye level with the edge. Sure enough, a small forward observation chopper meandered along, following the line of the road, barely thirty feet above it.

The rancher saw no markings, military or otherwise, and when it was close enough, he saw his old friend, Guapo, riding right seat with a rifle across his lap, scanning the road. Rand ducked back into the gulley and let the chopper pass and shower dust all over him. Immediately afterward, he climbed up to watch the aircraft continue north along the road until it suddenly stopped its forward motion and hovered.

The chopper turned west, elevated to a hundred feet, and ran about a mile before reversing and running a mile east past its initial pivot point. Then, the chopper turned north and made a wide arc, coming back around to the road again.

Somebody must have disagreed with Guapo's decision to leave the rancher alive. Rand ducked under a prickly pear growth and waited for the chopper to pass again.

The helicopter flew wide, lazy, circular search patterns, working its way south, basing its center on the road until it passed long away from his position, and Rand was about to leave his blind to take back to the road, but he thought the better of the move. He stayed hidden and was glad he did when the aircraft returned at high speed, hoping to catch a fleeing prey.

Smart, he thought. Ego's a killer, just like misplaced confidence. Had he been sure of the rifle he possessed, he would have risked the shot to kill the pilot, but he did not trust the weapon, so he allowed the helicopter to pass unmolested.

The rancher guessed that the helicopter had not chanced crossing into American airspace for more than a few minutes, so the border was only a mile or two away, hence his ranch was only twenty miles beyond that. Whether it was in a direct line or not was open to question. The ranch road was eighteen miles from the border, and it was a road he knew well. When he got to the road, he would know how much further it was to home.

Refreshed by the water, the rancher covered the mile and a half to the border in twenty minutes, hardly working up a sweat. The border was marked only by a barbed wire fence with a sign that said "Now Entering the United States" on its south face, and "Entrada de Mexico" on the north face. The wire was down on the dirt road to twenty feet on either side. Rand crossed the wire, feeling better to be back on American soil, but mindful that the helicopter could return at any moment.

He stood for a long moment, wishing for field glasses-- or better eyesight-- scanning for something familiar to guide onto for direction. The rancher wanted off the road, wanted more cover for the next fifteen miles. If these guys were smart, they'd be waiting for him somewhere along this dirt road.

Rand saw the mountain range in the distance and tried to gauge where he was, where the ranch was, in relation to his position. He opted to go north-northwest. It was now around ten, ten-thirty. If he pushed, he could meet the road by four. He knew where water troughs were near the road, so he could replenish there. He moved out, feeling strong.

The rancher followed a well-worn animal track for an hour and a half before he found a dead coyote, a male, and its tongue hanging out of its mouth. Another fifteen minutes on, and he found another one. This time a female at the edge of the trail, under a bush, with two dead pups still attached to her nipples as if suckling, but dead nonetheless. Rand noted the staggering paw prints that led to the body.

He continued for another thirty minutes and came upon a livestock tank, and it was just in the nick of time. The sun was high overhead, and he suspected he could drink the five hundred gallon tank dry, but something caught his eye as he neared the tank. On the far north side a half dozen horses lay on their sides, beyond them a few whiteface cattle in the same condition.

Rand knew this tank. He had watered here many times. He walked around the tank to take a look at the wellhead. It was broken off at the ground, rendered useless. He checked the water level, and it was good, but the dead livestock, coyotes meant only one thing. They had poisoned the tank.

The horses were not yet stiff, so they had used the tank less than three hours ago. It was bad news. The rancher wondered how many of the tanks had been poisoned. Good diversion, he thought. People would be so busy cleaning up; no one would look for anything else amiss.

It wasn't all bad news though. Rand now knew exactly where he was in relationship to his ranch, and he knew the shortest way to get there. On horseback, the trip was two hours, on foot, three or four.

He needed water, and it galled him to pull the skeg off the tank and let it empty, but he couldn't let anything else die from this. In the desert, water is the only thing worth more than money.

Rand now knew he could make it back to the ranch. Better still, he could make the butte if he went due north, but going to the ranch was habit. He turned north and worked his way toward the big arroyo that led to the stronghold.

Twenty minutes later, the rancher approached the familiar farm road that ran past his ranch. He had not realized how close he was because there was no traffic on it. Normally, one would see a truck coming one way or the other at this time of day, but now, nothing. He did not cross it immediately. He looked as far as he could see to make sure there was no ambush waiting. Since he was a half-mile east of the entrance to his property, the odds were good that anyone watching would have stationed himself closer to the entry.

Across the road, the terrain rose sharply to the top of the hill that backed his house on its east side. While it would be easier to skirt the western side of the hill, Rand chose to climb the hill. Knowing that the arroyo originated on the north side, he wanted the height to be able to check out the valley floor and the butte before entering the arroyo. The climb and crossing of the mesa would expose him for a short time; he weighted the recon more heavily than the risk.

When he reached the crest, Rand checked the farm road again. It ran flat for several miles until it cut through a cleft in a long ridge. While he could not see detail, he could see what appeared to be several vehicles stationed along both sides of the roadway. Aside from that, there was nothing unusual. He hoped it was the authorities, but the boast of Guapo made him leery of trusting anything.

The rancher crossed the five hundred yards of the mesa crest in a few minutes and was glad to be where he could see the butte. He approached the edge carefully, dropping to a crawling crouch near the edge.

Rand looked first down to his left at what remained of his house and stable. It had burned to the ground, and the roof lay on the hill like an upended tortoise. The Caddy and the truck were burned out hulks. The stable was a series of horseshoe shaped ash heaps and plastic lines where the fences had been. The horse carcasses had been ravaged by wild animals. He looked toward where the bedrooms had been and saw nothing resembling corpses.

The remains of the SUVs were gone.

He looked north and saw the full butte from top to bottom. There was nothing on the rock field, nor was there anything in the flats that surrounded the formation. To the northwest, the canyon he'd seen last night was vacant to the naked eye. It was time to move because he needed the water in the arroyo, if it was safe. Overhead, seven buzzards wheeled above the arroyo.

Rand found the narrow slit that eventually dropped into the arroyo. It was very steep at the top, leveling out as it widened. He started down, digging his heels in as he went, but six feet into it, he was forced to sit down and butt-skid for sixty or seventy feet until the

sand flattened into a shallow grade. It would have
been fun under other circumstances.

He met the bottom and rushed toward the stand of
salt cedars and water, hoping it wasn't poisoned like
the tank. There were no dead animals evident, so he
decided to chance it.

The water was warm and had the taste of minerals,
the same as he'd tasted just days ago. Had it been that
long?

After he drank, the rancher peeled off the scavenged
clothing and rinsed it out. He washed himself and
kept an eye on the buzzards above him. When he
finished, he wrung the clothing out and strung the
boots over his neck, the camo over his arm, and
began his wade toward the other end of the water. He
hoped to find again the place where he had
dispatched the three flankers and possibly to find a
useful weapon.

He considered that the flankers' compatriots had
recovered their bodies and had spirited them away. It
was not unreasonable to guess their bodies were
among those in the now burned out van, but digging
bodies out of tons of earth in a hurry was tedious at
best. He was near the site when he heard something
that surprised and delighted him at the same time.

From behind the stand of cedars, a soft nicker floated
toward the rancher. He slogged further and saw
Beamer standing in the shade on the bank. "Come
here, old boy," he spoke softly, and the draft horse
ambled over to him. They continued together to the

northern edge of the pond and mounted dry land near where the flankers had been covered.

The water in the pond had receded. The daylong rain did little to add to the volume. Rand checked to see if the bodies were still there. The least covered one was gone, but the earth above the other two was relatively undisturbed. Rand wouldn't have bothered, but he needed a more dependable weapon than the half melted piece he'd retrieved from Ysidrio. And he needed ammo.

A few minutes digging unearthed the body of the outermost man. Fortunately for the rancher, the man had fallen on the weapon and ammo bag, so it was easy to find. He found the man's canteen and some food rations, another plus. When he finished taking what he needed, Rand covered the body. He sat for a minute to clear the sand from the rifle, another AK, and then he stood to figure out whether to take Beamer with him to the stronghold.

The horse made the decision for him. As Rand walked north in the arroyo, the draft followed along next to him, waiting patiently when the rancher would scramble up to the arroyo rim to see if anyone followed. In less than an hour they reached the rock field.

The mid-afternoon sun beat down on them, but the draft gamely negotiated the field, remembering the way they had come. The rancher fretted that this exposure was foolish, that the crew that had caused them to climb up the chimney were still in the niche, but it was a risk he was willing to take. They crossed the field, either undetected or un-threatened, and reached the portal way.

Cool air descended from the stone hallway. Rand listened for any sound, and hearing nothing but breeze, he entered with his newly acquired AK ready to fire if needed. As he ascended, the draft followed like he'd done this all his life. The noise of his hoofs on the stone echoed up the shaft, and back again, sounding like a herd rather than one horse.

When the rancher reached the narrow, he heard the click of a safety and knew he had company. He hoped it was the right company.

"That you, El Paso?" Amy's voice sounded tired.

"Yes, ma'am," he responded. "You alone?"

"Two of us, if you count the Lord," stronger voice. "How 'bout you?"

"Two of us, if you count Beamer."

"Then come on up. I won't shoot."

A relieved Rand hurried up. He was glad to see the old woman, gladder than he'd ever been. "Where's Jim?"

She led Beamer into his stall, talking as she went. "He left early mornin' to go look for you. Said he was afraid you got blew up last night."

"What happened to the men who were here?" he indicated the niche.

She laughed. "Think I skeered'em away." She sat on a campstool. "I had a bad dream last night, like I sometimes do, and started yellin' down that hole there," she pointed at the chimney, "and alla sudden, they skedaddled like their rears were on fire." She laughed again. "Jim was skeered for a minute, and was gonna shoot 'em, but they were screamin' like a buncha scalded dogs. So he didn't"

"Then, I came down and he waited till we heard the explosions, and he went to see 'bout you."

"I'm sorry he left you alone." The rancher apologized.

"Oh, he didn't want to go, but I sent him. Not much backbone there," she grumbled. "Sure as hell not outta Texas. Hungry?" she asked.

He nodded, and the old woman busied herself finding food, muttering as she went. "They didn't find the food, nor the water. 'Pears to me they just sat and waited."

Rand ate while she continued. "What're you fixin' to do?"

"Gotta go back to the canyon. They did somethin' real bad down there, and I gotta figure out what to do," he answered, still not sure what he could do, but staying here was doing nothing, and he was unsure what the time frame was. Fourteen hours had passed since the explosions, and Guapo made it sound like things were in hurry-up mode.

"You still have the little crank up radio?" he asked.

"No, 'Worthless' took it with him. It was real staticky up here. Said he'd get better reception out in the flats. Prob'ly sittin' under a tree list'nin' to rock and roll."

Amy disappeared into the adobe and returned with pants and a shirt. "Best get out of those clothes. They're pretty gamy." While Rand changed, she found a pair of gym shoes. "These'll work better."

He was ready.

<u>Chapter Nine</u>

Whatever It Is, It Isn't Good

"Come back to me, you're all I've got," she murmured the last words. As Rand descended the ramp, he heard her continue softly, "You shall not dash your foot against a stone because His angels will bear you up, you shall not fear the fowler's snare...." Was all he heard, but he was certain she would keep going until she saw him again. It was her way. She had convinced Carol and the boy that she got answers. So much so that Carol and Chuck had developed the same habit.

It didn't bother the rancher. It did, however, remind him of the danger of the task at hand. He hoped she had prayed for Jim and that he would be able to find his heavyset ally. It was late afternoon, and Jim had been absent for ten hours.

Rand exited the portal way onto the rock field into the shade of the butte. He took a moment to check for any activity and found none, so he circled to the north side of the butte. Again, he scanned, and again, nothing. He trotted directly for the canyon.

In less than an hour, the rancher arrived at the mouth of the canyon. He passed the positions of the flats snipers, almost walked through a claymore trip wire that the gunmen had left behind. He took a moment to gather up the two pairs after removing the blasting caps. They were lighter than he remembered, all of them weighing less that the weapon he carried. He didn't know if he'd need them. In weaponry, more is always better than less.

The rancher got his first good look at the canyon. The blast had sheared of the sides to nearly vertical three quarters up the walls and had dumped the slough loosely all the way across the original canyon floor. The rims were untouched by the brunt of the explosion except here and there where large chunks broke loose and landed like big white pieces of eggshell on top of the loose dirt. The machinery, the bodies, the lights, everything else lay yards deep beneath the surface.

The back canyon rim looked much the same. The surface appeared to be cultivated and formed with a camouflage-look in mind. He could not see the fiberglass dome but was sure it was there, hidden, but there.

Rand dared not walk on the loose dirt for fear that the uncompacted soil would have voids where the equipment rested below. He opted for the same route he'd used last night and skirted north into the next, shallower canyon. The climb was easier by daylight. He saw where he started up and used the path, following his own footsteps. To his right, a bit deeper into the little canyon, he spotted two other sets of prints, made about the same time he made his.

The rancher realized he'd been followed. Halfway up the wall of the canyon, he stopped to check if he was now being followed, but he saw nothing. He continued to his climb-up place and poked his head above the rim. He was glad he looked because the sniper team had cleverly moved their claymores close to the rim, and he would have tripped the wire if he'd gone headlong over the rim.

Rand nodded his head at the craftsmanship, and disarmed the two closest mines, and made a mental note about the possibility of booby traps. It made sense. He jogged to the sniper station above the mouth of the canyon and disarmed the last two mines on the northern edge of the mesa, and then he walked to the edge and surveyed the bottom.

The demolition was good. There was no trace of what went on the nights before. The sun was already drying the surface soil. Another day of sun, and aerial observation would not detect the change. Rand walked west along the edge toward the end of the canyon where he'd observed the assembly of the cylinder. They had done a good job of covering it. He had a vague idea of where it was.

When Rand glanced back toward the mouth, he noticed a sinkhole above where the crane had been parked. It was big, maybe ten feet across, and sand around the edges collapsed into it as he watched. It didn't look right, so he backtracked to see if there was anything, like an antelope or coyote inside causing the continuing collapse. He arrived above the hole and peered inside.

Fifteen feet or so below the surface rim, the rancher could see a body moving, flailing, really, trying to climb out of the hole, but failing. One-step forward, two steps back, and the hole opening deeper behind the body. A closer look revealed that it was Jim trying to get himself out of a real fix.

"Hey," he called, and the sound of a human voice startled the heavyset man so badly that he fell, got to

his knees, fell again, then found footing and stood
with his hands high above his head.

"Stop moving around. You're just making it worse,"
Rand called down.

"That you, Rand?" Jim sounded exhausted.

"Yeah. How long you been down there?"

"All damn day. I came looking for you."

"Well, you found me. Stay put while I figure out how
to get you out of there."

Jim sat down. "Glad to."

The rancher walked along the rim to look for
anything that would help Jim out of the sinkhole, and
he found it. The detonator wire for the charges
remained intact except for where they joined the
primers. It took a few minutes, but Rand found
enough to braid together to get a line down to Jim. In
thirty minutes, the portly man half crawled, half crept
up the side of the sinkhole till he was within twenty
feet of Rand.

"Lay out as flat as you can and move west, the
ground'll get hard enough to walk on," he advised.
Sure enough, Jim's feet found purchase, and he
finally stood below Rand's position on the rim.

"You got any water," he asked, and Rand tossed him
a bottle.

The rancher believed they were thirty yards from the buried cylinder. He jumped off the rim and slid down to where Jim panted from the exertion.

"Don't move till I tell you to," Rand ordered. "If I guess right, this place is loaded with booby traps." He took out his assault knife and dug around, making a pathway to the presumed location of the silo. Jim stood back and waited, happy to be away from the sinkhole.

The rancher found two "Bouncing Betty" type mines, but closer to the cylinder was totally clear of anything but soil. He plunged the knife in slowly until he struck something six inches below the surface. He worked his way back, found the edge, and probed until he had the perimeter of the cylinder outlined. Rand called Jim to join him, and both scooped the sand cover away from the dome.

"Holy Mexican Jumping Beans, man. What the hell is this?" Jim queried.

"Their own private missile silo."

"So this is what it's all about," Jim sat straight down on the ground while Rand continued to dig to the bottom rim of the fiberglass cone. "I guess you haven't heard what's been going on in Texas and California?"

Rand stopped his excavation for a minute. "Been busy."

Jim produced the crank up radio, wound the spring load, and turned it on. "The cartels have been attacking the Federales and our Border Patrol. The Guard's been called out in both states and in New Mexico and here."

Then, the heavyset man took the lead digging out the other side of the cone as he recounted what happened after Rand left last night for the canyon.

"Your aunt and I stayed on the top and waited till you had cleared the rock field, then, for some reason, she started making howling noises down the shaft. I tried to stop her, but she kept at it, so I went over to guard where you told me. There was a lot of loud talk about "fantasmas" and "espiritas," then they started fighting among themselves, and a couple of guys left in a hurry."

He took a breath and restarted his digging. "I had a bead on them, but decided not to shoot and give our position away, and whaddaya know, the rest hauled out of there fifteen minutes later. We stayed put, thinking they might come back, but she wanted to go down, so I let her down on the rope, and stayed up there to keep an out for you.

"I got the radio to work, and heard what was happening on the border," he paused. "Not a word about Arizona." Jim returned to his digging. "What kinda missile is this?"

"Ever hear of an EMP?" Rand asked.

"Yeah. Nuclear or conventional?" Jim stopped dead.

"I dunno."

"Well, crap, ol' buddy. Wish you'da told me before we started this," Jim went back to his work. "We'll know in a few minutes, I guess." His voice trailed off.

"Tell me what you know," Rand's hand met the low edge of the cone and continued around the cylinder.

"Okay," Jim put on his best authoritative voice, as authoritative as it could be, considering he was digging dirt with his hands. "The original concept was to knock out communications by exploding a magnetic coil wrapped around an armature. It sends out an electro-magnetic pulse that fries electrical circuits.... everything from chips to wiring, and renders them useless."

Jim's hands reached Rand's trench, and both turned in their opposite directions to finish the trench. "Conventional weapons do it over a limited area, and it's cool because the blast demolishes hardware, but not people...in the main. It's still an explosion, but the frags are not dispersed over a wide area, so if you're far enough away, you don't get hit," he paused to wipe away sweat. "Man, this is the hardest I've worked in years." He breathed deep. "Of course, depending on the size, your cell phone goes to hell."

They finished the trench. Rand signaled, and they worked to lift the dome off the cylinder. It moved slightly, but it was heavier than either man expected. Jim noticed several dimples in the skin of the structure, which he pointed out to Rand. "See these indentations?" Jim ran his hand over them. "There's something under here. I'd guess it's some kind of electronics."

Rand told Jim that he'd seen a spiral shaped foil tape on the inside of the dome last night and what appeared to be plastic explosive in four lines from the point on the dome to the side where the cone joined the cylinder.

Jim sat straight down. His voice was exasperated. "Is there anything else about this that you want to tell me…. before we kill ourselves…and don't get any results?"

"We don't have time…" Rand protested.

"We better take it."

Jim then asked penetrating questions after Rand described exactly what he saw right down to the killing of the work crew and the cutaway explosion.

"Are you sure it was a solid propellant booster?" Rand nodded.

"How long was the missile body?"

"Thirty feet. Ten meters."

"How big a diameter"

When Rand answered, Jim swallowed hard. "Damn," was all he said.

Jim climbed up out of the trench and paced around the full circumference of the cylinder, his hand stroking his chin. "You were right about it being booby trapped. The plastic explosive serves double duty. It is supposed to blow the dome away pre-launch, but if it's messed with, kablooie." He raised his hands, palms down, like an explosion.

"I think the metal tape inside the dome that you described is an antenna, and it's smart because it can receive six different kinds of signals. I'm talkin' cell phone, satellite, shortwave. Like a fail-safe system. Idiot proof except for the people firing it."

He sat next to Rand and smoothed out a flat place in the sand. "Draw it."

"Think we got the time?"

"Hell, man…. we're dead men sittin' here if thing goes off. Draw like you're looking inside it. Everything you can remember, even if you don't think it's important."

Rand began with a small circle, but Jim stopped him. "This ain't notebook paper. You got the whole hill to draw on."

Rand drew what he'd seen, adding details as he remembered them. At length, he stopped and said, "That's all I can remember."

Jim stood to get the full picture. "More will come to you. Don't bother askin'; just draw it in when you think it. Now, draw the missile and framework…. big." Rand set to work on the next drawing, allowing Jim to study the dome drawing, which he did, muttering "Oh, crap, aw, hell."

He looked up from his concentration when Rand finished. "Damn good thing we didn't get that thing off when we tried."

"Why?"

"I believe we woulda launched this sucker."

It was about four o'clock. The shadow of the western rim of the canyon crept toward them and the dome. "We're losing daylight, and we gotta get a hole in this thing so we can look inside. I gotta see it before I can get a handle on what we gotta do."
Jim looked at the drawing of the missile and shook his head. "This can't be good."

He went back to the dome drawing and marked an X below the spiraling antenna tape. "Can you remember where the plastic was when it got set?" Rand shook his head.

"Okay, we need something non-metallic to tap on this thing."

Rand produced a water bottle, drank the contents, and filled it with sand. "This do?"

"It'll have to," Jim took the bottle and tapped on the dome at a low point. He couldn't hear well enough so he asked for a stick that he put to his ear and used as a stethoscope. He found a point and followed straight above, drawing a line in the dusty covering with his finger. He did the same thing three more times to locate the line of the shaped plastic explosive.

Jim went to the dimples he'd previously noted and tapped again till he found the outline of a box, which, again, he marked. He continued all around the dome, examining it carefully, marking every detail he could detect.

Meanwhile, Rand charred twigs and followed Jim's outlines until they finished. The painstaking process took an hour, and the portly man explained better to take the time now and regret it later than to hurry it and regret it immediately. They stood back and took stock.

"Anything else you remember?"

"Nope. Why didn't it go off in the explosions?"

"Damned if I know. I think it's designed to stay passive until it's called to life or tampered with. This is pretty sophisticated." Jim turned to the rancher. "Did you say some of these guys were Middle Eastern?" Rand nodded. "Guy said he'd lived here fifteen years. Said he went to MIT."

Jim stuck his jaw out. "Well, he wasn't smart enough to put this together by himself. This is missile you drew looks to be straight out of North Korea." He shrugged. "Guess we'll soon find out. Think that knife of yours can cut through this cap?"

"Reckon."

"Okay, let's start with a little hole about here." Jim pointed to a spot vacant of charcoal lines a few inches above the connection point at the cylinder and drew a small circle. As Rand began to work on the project, Jim once again used the stick as a stethoscope and listened. In a few minutes, Rand had penetrated the dome, and Jim knelt to look.

"Wow, it's light in there. Lit up like the Fourth of July…. pardon the expression." He went to Rand's dome sketch and marked numbers outside the circle between the lines that demarked the shaped plastic explosive, one through four, and quadrants.

"Okay. The charges are primed at the bottom." He pointed at the outside of the circle where the lines intersected the circumference. "The circuits look like they're buried in the charges and run to the electronics package…here." He touched the dome where they had outlined the dimples. "Then, there's a cable (which you forgot to mention to me) that attaches from the electronics package to a port on the missile. I suspect that the ignition package is a built-in."

"How do you know about this stuff?" Rand asked.

Jim sketched another box near the bottom of the dome and replied "Subscription to Janes' magazine."

"Okay. Cut here, but do it gently. The circles of tape," he paused. "I think they're charged. If they break, it could set up the launch sequence."

Rand knew from his earlier experience how to cut through the fiberglass. He used the serrated spine of his assault knife and sawed as quickly as he dared through the material. He removed the square sheet and tossed it aside. Jim took off his watch and used a twig to lower it carefully into the dome. He let it sit on level with the nose package of the missile for a moment and withdrew it.

Jim showed the watch face to his companion. The numerals glowed brightly. "Well, one thing we know…it's a nuke." He stretched and sat down. "We need some smoke."

Rand retrieved green mesquite branches from the rim, lit them above the hole he'd made in the dome, and blew the resulting smoke inside. No explanation was necessary. He looked inside and saw what Jim suspected. The smoke trailed down along the launching frame and was cut in the tiers by red beams of light that passed on all four sides of the missile. It was an alarm system.

Jim confirmed what Rand thought. "Yup. Thank God, there's no vertical axis on these things."

The sun was now so low that most of the canyon was in the shadow of the rim. In two hours, it would be dark. Jim sat next to the sand drawings and contemplated his next move.

"Here's what I think. There's probably two power supplies to this puppy. One that operates the passive system that waits for a signal to activate. This system operates the security system and the passive response. If the security system is breached, or if it receives a wake up command, the first power supply activates the launch sequencing system by hitting the second power supply with a jolt kinda like priming a pump, or using jumper cables.

"The fact that it has two power systems, one always on, means that the life of this equipment is finite. Lasers burn juice, the passive system burns juice, and even though it's really low power expenditure, it can run out, and one of two things can happen. A low power volume can trigger a launch sequence, or it can simply die.

"These guys are serious about this. I believe low juice will cause an automatic launch sequence."

Rand looked askance. "Why?"

"Depending on the yield of the device, they could hurt us real bad."

"How bad?"

"Real bad. This missile is real fast. It hits mach one in thirty seconds. Mach two in one minute. That means in three minutes it's reached a detonation point that would eliminate the most of the western power grid. In seven minutes it would take out everything west of the Mississippi. In fifteen minutes, the entire United States. No deaths, just no power.... anywhere."

Rand considered. "No response time."

"None. And nobody knows it's here but us."

"And the bad guys," Rand reminded him.

Jim let the gravity of the situation settle in. "You think they'll come back?"

"If my plan didn't come together, I would," Rand answered, and he considered for a full minute before he added, "Probably won't be the same guys."

"Meaning?"

"Meaning whoever they bought will show up."

"How will we know?"

"It'll be the first guys to come here. Right here without stopping anywhere else. They'll come down the wash. Could be a lot." Rand let the words trail off. Then he asked, "Can we kill this thing?"

"Yeah. We can kill it. It may kill us first."

"What's the plan?" Rand asked.

"Reckon we gotta get past the booby traps first. Then we can see how to disable it or destroy it."

It was dusk. The rancher pulled a mini flashlight from his vest and prepared for night duty. Jim went back to the drawings and refreshed his memory of what he'd seen. The two men took an inventory of things at hand. The heavyset rancher had never seen a claymore mine for real, but he did recall reading about them on the Internet. Rand, on the other hand was very familiar with them.

Jim marked three more rectangles for Rand to cut so one of them could release the ignition caps from the plastic explosive. It they were lucky, there was no redundancy in these, but each strip would have to be checked for such. Since Rand's arms were longer, it was he who took the assignment.

Reaching inside the dome through the cut holes, Rand first removed each cap of fulminate of mercury from its embedment, pulled it outside, and under the light of the mini, he disconnected its wires. He set each cap near the drawings and moved to the next port. The rancher discovered that the plastic explosive strips detached easily from its dome placement, so he removed all four and set them opposite the caps. He left the exposed wires dangling from the ports.

Jim re-examined the drawings and added little marks that signified gained knowledge. Rand had to admit to himself that the heavyset guy had value. He was glad he'd pulled the man from the sinkhole.

Jim took the mini-light and peered into the dome from the nearest port. "Okay, there's two main cables. One's attached to the nose cone…probably both guidance and arming. I read somewhere that these things are designed with a pre-guidance system in place so no matter what happens, this thing already knows where it's going, but it's too tricky to arm the warhead until it clears the silo."

Rand asked, "Can the warhead go off before it leaves?"

"Not usually. Why kill off your techs on a misfire? My opinion is that while they modified the warhead for this application, they probably didn't want it to go off prematurely. My bet's on arming after the missile has cleared launch. If it went off before thirty-mile altitude, all they would get is a bunch of cooked cell towers, and it would blow their cover. Arming is either on a timer or aneroid barometer, and that's good for us."

"You pretty sure 'bout that?"

"No, does it make a difference?" Jim was trying to be funny, but the tension in his voice gave him away.

He went back to his inspection of the interior of the dome and silo, crouching beside the cylinder. "Hello, Mama," Jim said out loud. He looked at the electronic array at the top inside of the dome. He motioned for Rand to have a look as well. "'Member I was talking about redundancy?" he shined the light for Rand. "See that little bracket on the side of the yellow box with all the little lights? See that thing attached to the bracket?" Rand nodded. "Well, pal, there's our redundancy. It's a the frickin' guts to a sat phone."

Jim was all excited to see it. "Talk about dial up connections…just like IEDs in the war zone. These guys haven't changed at all." He sat back and gloated. "Best part about it is that the SIM card is sittin' out in the open because they were too cheap to use a battery. They got it hooked up to the main power supply." He stood up and looked again at the diagram.

"Think we can lift this dome off a bit?" he asked. When Rand looked doubtful, Jim reassured him. "All we gotta do is move it far enough so I can get up inside of it. We're not takin' anything loose yet. I wanna get the SIM card out of the sat phone."

Rand leaned over and hefted one edge of the fiberglass shape. It felt like it weighed about the same as a light boat. "Yeah, I think we can."

"Okay," Jim responded, and the two worked their way around the dome, lifting a few inches at a time, very much like getting the lid off a paint can. They placed rocks against the steel silo as they moved. In two circuits, they were within a half-inch of lifting it off. Jim took one more look inside from each port to satisfy himself that there were no more booby traps or snags.

"Let's go.... very easy and slow," Jim urged. Rand, on the opposite side lifted in unison, and the dome came free. They let it rest on the cylinder, and under Jim's direction moved it until it rested, balanced on the steel silo. "Can you hold it for a minute?" Jim asked. "Till I get something under the open side?" Rand shuffled his handhold to the very outside and grunted that he could. Jim shoved dirt down until Rand could rest the dome at a sight slant.

On his hands and knees, Jim crawled under the open edge of the dome. Rand looked inside from the nearest port and watched his neighbor examine the now available inside of the dome. It was tall enough that Jim could kneel upright.

"Gotta first aid kit?" his voice echoed off the dome and into the silo.

Rand had a little survival kit for which he clawed around in his vest. When he produced it Jim called out for tweezers or, better yet, cotton swabs. "If the tweezers are metallic, give me the swabs."

Jim reached to the cradle and used the swabs to extract the SIM card from the sat phone. "Okay, one down. One or two to go," he sighed. "You realize they could be using the sat phone to run diagnostics or to keep tabs on their little machine here," he said more to himself than to anybody else. "If they are, they'll know we're here."

Rand was ahead of Jim on that score. Jim crawled out from under the dome with the SIM card between his thumb and index finger. Rand held the mini light while Jim snapped it in half, then once more, then both men leaned over the open part of the silo and took their first good look at the missile.

"Oh, yeah," Jim mused. "North Korean all right." He shined the light down the sides of the missile body. "Left the peninsula in a lotta pieces. Probably assembled in a warehouse south of here. You can see the pieces bolted together. Very simple."

He examined the egg shaped nosepiece. "This is all breakaway stuff. Made to come apart in light atmosphere. See these lines here?" His light traced seams that ran from the very top down to the point where it attached to the missile body. "Glued together. Super Glue. Would you believe it?" He directed the light beam to the fattest part of the "egg" and played up and down. "In here, armor plate of vanadium steel, wrapped around the explosive and disrupter material. Zero penetration."

Jim directed the beam to the joint assembly. "This here is the weakest part, but that ain't sayin' a lot. There could be a separation package in there that blows it off the body for detonation, but I'm just not sure..." his voice trailed off.

"Can we dismantle it?" Rand bent to inspect it.

"Wouldn't do much good. Those things gotta weigh six or seven hundred pounds. We couldn't lift it if there were six of us."

Chapter Ten

This Isn't as Easy as It Looks, Is It?

Rand straightened up. "How do we kill it?"

"Well, we could disable the nozzles. But if we try to hit it at the top of the body, just under the warhead assembly point, it could just turn the whole damn thing on because that's where the igniters are…at the very top." He directed the light beam lower, picked up a handful of fine sand, and sprinkled it down the shaft where it was lit up by the red laser beams some eight feet below the rim of the silo.

"If we can get a hole in the side, drain off some of the propellant. It's like a bunch of ball bearings, and it takes a lot of heat to ignite it, but it's real stable and doesn't burn unless the high temperature maintains to get it to flashpoint." Jim looked to Rand for a method.

"Can we disable the warhead package?"

"Maybe. It's set off by a high explosive charge that gets it to fission temperature before the chain reaction starts, but I'm thinking that we can get a hole in the side of the missile body, it won't matter because it will shoot the gases sideways and the rocket will destroy itself." Jim bit his lip. "There's one problem though. Once this propellant starts to burn, it can't be stopped."

"And?"

"If it reaches temperature, it could set off the device. We'd be toast." Jim said with finality. "Toast."

Rand considered the problem. His analysis was that the primary goal was to keep the missile from lifting off either by breaching the fuel container or by wrecking the nozzle system. The drawback was that the resulting fuel fire could set of the warhead device. The secondary goal was to interrupt the warhead device and keep it from its purpose. He asked Jim to sketch a cross section of the missile body and another of the "egg."

Then Rand asked Jim to point out the sections he'd described in the drawings on the missile and on the egg. While Jim explained, Rand thought about how to disable both. The problem was like a Woody Allen quote when he said "The idea of dying doesn't really bother me. I just don't want to be there when it happens." It was a close corollary to the problem the two ranchers faced.

Rand knew he could blow this sucker up, knew he could stop it, but he wasn't equipped to do it remotely. The claymores he'd collected from the snipers' positions had enough firepower to breach the missile's fuel containers. The plastic explosive he'd retrieved from the dome could pop the warhead off the missile. Ignition of the nuclear primer was another question. He couldn't answer it.

"How you feelin'?" Rand asked Jim.

"Why?"

"Think you can make it back to the butte?"

"I think so. How fast?"

"Fast."

Rand assessed their chances. He formulated an idea using the tactics the designers of this system had created. The seeds of the solution are always inside the problem, he remembered someone saying, and if there were ever an occasion, this was it.

Jim was thrashed. He breathed heavily and sat on the edge of the ditch next to the silo. "What do you want to do?"

Rand shined the mini light onto the connecting point between the egg and the missile body. "If we separate the nose assembly from the missile body with the plastic, what do you think will happen?"

Jim thought a moment. "Well…it could detonate, or it could just fall off and roll down the hill. Or it could fall off, roll down the hill, then go off, but if it did, the pulse wouldn't damage much because we're sittin' in a geological depression. I'd hate to be in an airliner above it when it went off."

"How long?"

"Seconds, maybe a minute. These things don't arm that quick for personnel safety reasons. Why?" Jim stood and looked into the silo.

The top of the egg was about three feet below the upper rim of the metal silo, and its attaching collar was three feet below that. Rand surmised it was going to be tricky, but he had to chance it. He directed the mini's beam back toward Jim's cross-section of the egg and missile. "Show me the weakest point, farthest away from the nuke's primer."

Jim sketched a line a couple of inches above the attachment point. "Any lower and there's a risk of igniting the solid fuel primer."

"Okay, show me where you want the hole to siphon off the propellant."

Jim took the mini light and directed its beam to a point eighteen inches below the attachment point. "The primer is most likely in a bladder or soft tank that sits on top of the propellant. The solid fuel in kinda stacked in tiers with the most energetic on the top to overcome the rocket's inertial. It is formed around a starburst shaped cavity that ensures even burning, but usually these North Korean jobs aren't that perfect. They don't have enough petroleum products like epoxy for anything but the cavity formation. Outside the cavity, the fuel looks more like loose rabbit pellets, so it'll pour out like BBs. The big deal is to breach the side of the body so that the thrust comes out perpendicular to the axis of the missile."

"What will happen/" Rand focused on the missile.

"Prob'ly won't get out of the silo. If it does, the whole thing will keystone, tumble end over end. Totally out of control."

Rand had heard enough. He hoped Jim knew what he was talking about. "What kind of sat phone is that?"

"Cheap Nokia." Jim stated flatly.

"You think it has a time alarm on it?"

"I can check" He crawled under the dome to look. "Yup." His voiced echoed down the cylinder.

"Can you reset it?"

"Easy."

"Okay. Can you string the wires out enough to reach me?"

"Nope."

"How much you got?" Rand groped in the dark for the wires he'd removed from the dome charges, and Jim came out from beneath the dome. The light helped but Rand knew he did not have enough. He took the light and scuttled downhill toward the sinkhole from which he'd pulled Jim. The rancher gathered up the wire scavenged from the wall explosives and hurried back up the hill to the top of the silo, wire in hand.

The wire was standard household two-wire, each length twenty feet, the ends fused by the heat of the explosions, which brought down the walls of the canyon the night before. Rand found six lengths, three he'd braided together to rescue Jim who now awaited his arrival at their "work" site.

The rancher dug near the outer wall of the silo and unearthed one of the attachment rings that had been used to lift the steel into place. He tied the already braided wires to the open ring and let the loose end dangle into the silo. It landed on one of the frame's crossbars near one of the security lasers. Rand tested the strength of the braid and was satisfied it would bear his weight.

"Scoop out enough dirt so we can move the dome farther off the silo," he ordered. "You'll be inside guy, okay?" To which Jim nodded and crept around the silo to perform the task. Meanwhile, Rand sat next to the strands of plastic explosive he'd earlier removed from the inside of the dome. He gathered it all up and twisted it together. The night air had cooled considerably, and the chill stiffened the material, making it harder to knead, so the rancher put the coil inside his vest to warm it.

Finished with the excavation, Jim sat and rested, watching his neighbor work on the wire. Rand used the assault knife to cut two of the remaining wires into ten-foot lengths and stripped the ends, staggering the cuts six inches. He then spliced one set to two blasting caps, again staggering the splices because he had nothing with which to insulate them. He set this module aside and motioned that Jim was not to touch them. He created one more splice set on the last wire, again adding two caps to the end.

Rand then removed the plastic from inside his vest and kneaded it carefully together, rolling it between his palms to achieve a uniform thickness of two inches, six feet long. He coiled it up like a lasso and set it near where Jim would be working. He gathered up two of the claymore mines and stuffed them into his shirt. He checked to see that he still had the primer caps in his pocket. He did.

Jim sensed that Rand was ready to descend into the silo. He picked up a handful of sand and sifted it into the silo to reveal the laser beams that monitored the missile's security. The beams crossed immediately above the framework crossbars, some two feet beneath the point Jim had designated as the desired breach. Four lasers crossed the silo like chords that sat two inches to the missile body. Rand thought it was actually kind of pretty, or would be if they didn't represent such danger.

The two men pushed the dome as far to the side as they could without losing access from the dome to the silo. While Jim crawled under the edge and into the hollow of the dome, Rand opened the first aid kit and extracted a pitifully small roll of surgical tape. He handed the mini light to Jim and readied himself to descend into the silo.

"How ya doin'?" he called out to his neighbor as he climbed over the rim and let his feet down to the crossbar.

All he heard back was "Uh oh."

"I hate the sound of that." Rand balance on the crossbar. It was spongy, and it flexed as he moved around on it, making the laser beams waver. He stilled himself and spoke to Jim. "What?"

"The lights are flashing all different. It's either sequencing to fire, or…." Jim halted for a moment. "Or it's checking…or someone is."

"What's it mean?" Rand held his breath.

"We should hurry." Jim's voice was tense. "I mean, like…hurry."

Rand swiveled, found his balance, and called for the plastic rope he'd fashioned. Jim handed it down. Rand used the braided wire to help him lean across the space between the silo side and the missile. He touched the skin of the egg for the first time. It was ceramic, a good thing. He applied the rope in a circle that reached all the way around the narrow neck under the egg. He pushed hard to make it adhere to the cold surface. It held.

"Okay," Rand, relieved that the plastic had found purchase, called up to Jim in a voice louder than it needed to be because his partner was only a few feet away. "Set the timer on the sat phone, then when you're sure, splice in the cap wires, and let the caps down to me…gently."

"What time shall I set?"

"Well, barring the unforeseen, we need another ten minutes here, then we gotta get back to the butte…. inside. Say two hours."

Jim set the phone alarm, spliced the wires, and let down the caps. Rand had not moved. He took one cap and set it into the plastic, then reached around as far as his arms would go, and set the remaining cap.

"Now splice in the long line and drop it to me." Rand strung the braid around his chest and stepped off the crossbar, letting the line bear his weight. He let down a little, being careful not to interrupt the laser sentries. He tied himself off when his chest lined up with the point where Jim said was under the solid fuel ignition charge. He retrieved one of the claymores from inside his shirt and held it next to the silo wall. The rancher produced the surgical tape and used it to attach the mine to the wall. He repeated the operation just below the one he'd placed and called for the long wire.

Jim dropped the end and called out excitedly. "Man, these lights are going nuts." Rand set the caps in the built-in ports on the mines and spliced the long wire to the cap leads.

"Time to go," he said, and it took no time for Jim to come out from under the dome. Rand's toes found the crossbar again, and he stood, facing the silo wall. Jim grabbed the braid and hauled away, giving Rand the boost ne needed to reach the top of the silo. He hoisted himself over the top, rolled across it, and landed on his side.

Jim moved toward the downhill side of the silo, and Rand stopped him. "Can't go home that way." He gathered up his bag, handed his partner a bottle of water, taking one for himself. "We go this way," indicating the rim of the canyon. They climbed the ten yards to the canyon rim. The mini flash flickered, and then died.

Both men were sweaty and tired, but they labored on, turning south at the rim and hiking the eastward arch until they came to where Rand remembered the position of the southeast sniper team. He put his hand on Jim's chest to stop him, the got on his hands and knees to feel around for a trip wire.

This mine he left after having turned it slightly to face the end of the ridge. He reset the trip wire so that it would cross to the rim. He groped more and found the last mine, which he rearranged to cover more to the south. Then he guided Jim around the kill zone till they came to the easternmost rim that faced out toward the flats.

They descended the hill and came to the desert floor. Rand moved ahead of his partner to enter the wash first and to check for intruders. Jim's nervousness at the light display had its effect on the rancher, since the missile had not gone into launch mode. It was a good bet that the bad guys had run a diagnostic on the installation. Even if the answer came back to them as inconclusive, they would have to lay eyes on it.

He was dog-tired, and he knew Jim was beyond exhausted, but they were down to the last minutes. They crossed the wash and took the meandering animal path toward the rock field. Jim stumbled along, doing his best, and Rand felt bad for him, but there was no time for sentiment.

When they reached the rock field, Rand felt more at ease. Almost there, he thought. Forty-five minutes had elapsed since they'd left the silo. He knew they could make it in time. If the nuke went off, they'd be inside the niche that faced away from ground zero.

Another twenty minutes transpired, and the two men were at the portal that led to the stronghold. Jim found new energy for climbing the stairway, but when he reached the niche, he collapsed onto the rock floor unceremoniously. Rand went directly to a cistern and dowsed himself generously with the cold water.

"Y'all back okay?" Amy's voice came from inside the small adobe.

Rand answered "By the skin of our teeth."

"Y'all must be starved. 'After eating and being filled praise the Lord.' What can I get you?" Amy was once more the teenager from East Texas.

Jim rolled over on his back and moaned something about his watch, but it made no sense. When Rand did not respond, Jim forced himself to sit up. "I set the timer on my watch. Forty-five minutes left." He took food from Amy and ate it down in minutes.

Rand ate on the move. He located another mini flash and used it to find the .50 and the crank up radio. "I'm goin' up on top. Wanna come?" he asked Jim who practically had to scrape himself off the floor to go to the chimney. Amy helped with water and the weaponry bag.

"Y'all go on up. I'll tie this stuff on for you. 'Tears last for a night, but joy cometh in the morning.' Be careful up there." She went to her place in the small adobe, cooing soothing words to the draft that fed happily on his hay.

When Jim finally joined Rand on the top of the butte, he lifted the field glasses and peered for a long moment toward the canyon while Rand prepped the

.50 and set it on it bipod at the ready to the southwest. The portly rancher handed the glasses over to his partner and said "I've got blast covers for the lenses if you want to watch the fireworks. They automatically darken."

Rand took the glasses and looked first at the canyon, then zoomed the view out to check the highway to the west as far as the cleft where it disappeared into the hillside. He scanned due south and noticed something, although he was not sure what it was. Behind him, Jim cranked the radio to charge its power supply, and then he turned it on.

"Hey, I got the BBC." He put the earpiece in and listened intently. After a moment, he became agitated. "Holy Moley.... oh, wow...oh, wow." He sat down and began to rock back and forth. "Well, if there was ever a reason to set up a stealth weapon inside the continental United States, this was it."

Chapter Eleven

This Can't Be Good

Rand was only paying half attention to Jim's rant. "Incoming," he stated, looking south through the glasses. As he spoke the word, Jim heard the sound of a helicopter approaching over the wash. It crossed the highway and lights switched to life on its undercarriage. The aircraft slowed as it wallowed side to side as if inspecting the ground beneath it.

The helicopter hovered, moved forward, hovered. "How much time we got?" Jim checked his watch. "I make it ten, fifteen minutes at the outside." The aircraft advanced halfway down the wash toward the canyon, then it suddenly rose straight up, the lights switched off, it turned and flew toward the highway.

"That's weird," Jim stood. "What just happened?"

Rand pointed to the southwest. "Waitin' for re-enforcements." In a moment four sets of vehicle lights appeared a couple of miles away. "They were running dark for a while."

"How many?"

"Sixteen at best, two dozen at worst, plus two in the chopper. It ain't good," Rand grumbled. "What'd the BBC say?"

"Egypt, Syria, Lebanon have massed troops on the Israeli borders. Iran threatened the U.S, with an attack that would make 9/11 look like an ice cream social. But the attacks on the Mexican border just melted like nothing ever happened. The President wouldn't allow our people to give chase into Mexico."

The vehicles massed on the highway beneath the helicopter for a moment. The chopper lifted and turned on its belly lights. It advanced north along the wash, and the vehicles below it came alive with code four lights as they followed, bouncing along the wash.

Jim became very excited. "Finally, the cavalry rides in to the rescue," he paused, the said "Hey, we gotta warn them." He picked up the mini light and was about to signal them when rand stopped him.

"These aren't friendlies."

"But they're official cars."

"Not friendlies. Remember what I told you at the site? That they'd go directly to the site? These guys know exactly where it is. Friendlies wouldn't." Rand ambled over to the west side of the butte. "How's our time?"

"Five minutes."

"We gotta get ready."

"Why?"

"'Cause they'll come here next." Rand spoke too soon. The helicopter veered right and flew straight for the butte at the height of the niche. The rancher saw outlines of little protrusions next to the lights.

Rockets. He ran to get the .50, grabbed it and rolled toward the southern perimeter of the butte crest.

The aircraft hovered fifty yards off the face of the butte and directed its lights into the niche. Rand fired the .50 down once, and the slug penetrated the Plexiglas pod, striking the left seat man with so much force that it tore him out of his seat, and pitched him away from the chopper. He racked another round and fired again, hitting the right seat man mid chest. The helicopter jerked backward and pitched up, firing a missile that passed over Rand's head, running wild into the night. Then the aircraft fell backward straight to the rock field and exploded.

Meanwhile, the line of cars had pulled up to the mouth of the canyon, the doors flung open, and men not caring about the dome lights, spilled out of the vehicles, running for the canyon. Rand joined Jim on the western rim. "Might want to get down," Rand pressed Jim toward the ground. "Never know." They saw flashlights play the ground at the mouth of the canyon, indicating the progress of the ground party.

Rand was about to ask if Jim's watch could be wrong when a brilliant flash of light shot vertically from the silo. Above the light, the egg shot up a hundred feet, lit from the bottom by the fire in the silo. It appeared to hang in the air for a second, and then, it lost momentum and fell back toward the canyon. There was another burst of light that illuminated the landscape from the interior of the canyon to high above the rim.

The missile burst forth from the silo. Below the missile an inverted torch flared out, and from its side flame spilled forth like a cascade of light. The resulting illumination revealed the egg landing on the downhill side of the silo, bouncing and rolling toward the mouth.

The two men heard the report of the first explosion before the missile fell in a lazy, spinning arc toward the ground above the canyon rim. The skin of the missile fractured, bleeding the fuel like a spray and igniting as it splayed across the wreckage. The sound of the wounded missile, and its death throes arrived and finished shortly after the fire settled into a flat line of red and yellow light.

Rand and Jim observed the regrouping at the vehicles and were able to discern the men's weaponry and equipment. "How many?" Rand asked.

"I make out sixteen…give or take," Jim answered. "They're wearing police uniforms, Rand."

"They're not cops."

Rand took the field glasses and surveyed the group below. The group of men assembled near the vehicles, giving Rand to get a good count. There were eighteen individuals, and they were very interested in the butte. He judged they were aware of the helicopter crash, and were none too happy about it. The rancher was puzzled that the group made no immediate move toward the butte.

He stood and moved toward the chimney, speaking as he went. "I'm going back down, but I need you to keep an eye on these guys, and let me know when they move." Jim was in agreement.

"You want me to shoot?"

"Only when they get to the rock field, but remember to shoot, move, shoot, move like I told you. Aim center mass. No matter what you hit, you'll disable them. Don't forget that these guys want us dead. You've seen what they're capable of." With that, Rand descended into the chimney.

Amy was waiting for him when he reached the floor of the niche. "What was that all about?" she asked. Rand explained to her about the explosion, but she was more interested in the helicopter crash, so he said he thought they had a mechanical problem, and let it go at that.

Since they already knew where they were, the rancher decided to get some light on the situation. He found one of Jim's camp lights and turned it on. It was time to take inventory.

In his weaponry bag, he still had four claymores. Rand rushed into the portal way and set a tripwire where the narrow place broadened facing the kill zone down. He stacked the three remaining mines near the point where the pathway veered to enter the niche. He considered setting one at the opening to the small adobe, but he rejected the idea because of Amy. No telling where she might wander when he snuffed the light.

The rancher pulled out everything Jim had stockpiled. The AK was still serviceable, and he had enough ammo to load four magazines, a hundred and twenty rounds. There were maybe twenty more loose rounds. He checked the Sig. He re-loaded the mag it held and loaded two more that he stashed in vest. He used a smooth stone to hone the blade on the assault knife. The work on the dome had taken a toll on the edge.

It was time to east, drink, and rest. Rand retrieved an MRE and stationed himself on a camp chair under the chimney. Amy drew a camp chair over next to him, put her hand on his shoulder, and spoke under her breath. He knew she was praying. As soon as he finished eating, he fell asleep sitting up.

Rand woke up in the dark; the old woman still had her hand on his shoulder. Amy had not awakened him; Jim's voice from above was what stirred him. "They're on the move."

"Which way?" Rand called back.

"Looks like they split into two groups. Half going north and half going south."

"Can you get a shot?"

"No. They're staying out of the rock field. What do you want to do?"

"Gimme a minute." Rand thought. He checked his watch. It was four. "Can you get a position on the east end?"

"Wait a sec." He came back in a few minutes. "It's rugged. Won't be able to hit and run, but I have a good place."

"Do it. They're gonna come in at the closest point on the north side, hug the butte, then make for the passageway. If you can't shots when they cross, you can shoot straight down over the passage. Got it?" Rand hope he was right and that Jim understood.

"Got it."

Thirty minutes passed, and Jim returned to call down the chimney. "They're just sittin' there."

The message worried Rand. His experience told him that assault teams wait for nothing but backup. He wondered if there were more intruders on the way, or worse if there was more firepower on the way.

He didn't have to wait long for the answer. The sound of a heavy helicopter beat the air of the southern approach. Rand could tell it was coming in loaded. It was still too dark to make out what type, but the fact was that whatever was coming in was better than what had he'd sent to the base of the butte a few hours ago, and the only weapon in his inventory that stood a chance against an armored chopper was on the top of the butte with an inexperienced rifleman.

Bringing down any helicopter with less than an RPG was tough. An armored chopper was three times harder to disable, let alone destroy. Rand dashed to the outer edge of the niche and lifted two of the claymores, unraveling the igniter cords as he crept to the very rim. He felt along the solid rock and found a long, narrow crevice that ran out from the passageway to the western wall. He unfolded the middle stake leg of one and pressed it hard into the crevice. He tilted the angle so the blast would fire in line with the horizon. He tossed the trigger behind him and set the ignition cap into its port.

The rancher then took the other mine and moved east along the rim, his fingers following the crevice until it sealed, twenty feet away from the first mine. He drove the stake in until it held, and then, he focused its angle ten degrees above the horizon. He hoped the chopper would come in close enough for the mines to, if nothing else, blind it. The range on these things was not all that good, but these guys were pissed, and they would make mistakes.

Rand needed them to make one more big mistake.

Amy picked up the triggers, which scared Rand more than anything that had happened so far. She handed them to the rancher and toddled off toward the small adobe to comfort Beamer. "You shall not fear the arrow that flies by day, not the pestilence that walks by night," her voice echoed off the granite walls of the stronghold.

"It's not the arrows I'm worried about." He said grimly.

Jim called down once again. "What's happening?"

"Concentrate on the assault group. Keep out of sight of the chopper."

The eastern sky grayed, and Rand could see the chopper as a black thing that threatened the valley floor. He discerned that it was indeed armed and armored equipment, Vietnam era surplus. He could tell it was overloaded by the way it lugged across the landscape. It flew very low, skimming the tops of the mesquite dunes with less than ten feet to spare.

The helicopter came straight in toward the niche, homing in on the wreckage at the base of the butte. Rand decided the pilot was a real hot shot who had never been in combat. It appeared this guy would do a Blue Thunder move, flying in close to the base, then elevating along the wall until he was on level with the niche. The rancher bet that this guy would rack off non-stop until he sprayed the place with all the lead he had.

Ego's a killer, he thought.

Sure enough, the chopper did come up exactly as he had suspected, and he was close to the wall, the rotors less than five feet in the clear. Rand backed off to take cover behind the protrusion of rock on the west side of the niche. Not that it mattered, the ricocheting lead would probably kill him anyway, but old habits die-hard. As he took cover he noticed rock and sand falling from above the niche and thought "Dammit, Jim." He saw something hit the tail rotor, saw it split off, saw the tops of the rotors rock violently, and then he saw the helicopter spin violently toward the wall of the butte.

The chopper glanced off the wall ten feet below where Rand stood, the rotors buckling as they struck the granite. The engine wound way out, screaming all the way to the rock field and making a loud crunching sound as it met the ground.

The rancher looked over the edge in time to see the fuel tanks rupture and explode, but there was no time to waste, and this was no time to waste materiel. He raced to the first claymore and cranked it over to cover the passageway, bending the setting stake is his rush. He completed the same operation with the second when he heard the .50 go off above him. The ground assault was underway.

Rand found the AK and stationed himself above the passageway. He heard another report from the .50, and then he heard return fire echoing up the passageway. He stretched up and saw an arm swing into the portal at the very bottom, then a grenade, poorly thrown, made it halfway up. The rancher ducked and waited till it went off. It was only the first.

There was more automatic rifle fire. Rand assumed it was an attempt to keep Jim down. He peeked up again and spotted one brave soul inside the passageway with a grenade ready. The man tossed it, but it bounced off the wall at the wide spot and tumbled back down the ramp. The thrower turned and ran, but Rand hit him, and ducked in time.

"How many?" he shouted to Jim.

"I got three," the .50 went off again. "Make that four."

"Thirteen to go," Rand thought out loud. He shouted up to Jim, "How many can you see?" Smoke from the burning chopper burned his eyes.

There was no sound of movement from the passageway. Rand chanced a look. The sun was just up, so he could see shadows below, and he waited for more grenades. Jim's voice came from above, "I count eleven."

"Can you get a shot?"

"Nah, they're huggin' the wall."

"Come on down."

"Okay."

Eleven. Rand wondered, "Where are the other two?" The heat from the fire below became more intense; the smell of burning flesh didn't make it any better. The rancher racked his brain. Jim emerged from the chimney hole at the back of the niche, and Rand motioned him over to his position. "Keep your eyes peeled for grenades. They're up to something."

The rancher crossed toward the little adobe to check on Amy. She sat in the dark, humming "Jesus Loves Me" over and over. He grabbed two water bottles and tossed one to Jim. Then, he realized where the other two were. He rounded the corner and pulled the Sig from his waist. He neared the small opening to the latrine and peeked inside.

Whoever was in the hole he'd used earlier had arrived, but he had not revealed himself, then, the intruders hands filled with a Mac 10 came up over the ledge. Rand saw the fingers tighten on the grip. He fired the Sig at the weapon and scored a hit with the first shot, hit the hands with the second shot. A man screamed and cursed, then Rand heard the clink of a grenade latch bouncing down the hole. It popped up over the ledge, and Rand dived for it. He caught it and tossed it back down the hole as he ducked away from the blast zone.

It went off, spewing fragments up from the latrine hole. At the very same moment, a barrage of gunfire erupted from the direction of the passageway and the two grenades went off. Rand peered out through the smoke and made out Jim, hugging the floor. From the passageway there was shouting and continuing automatic fire.

Rand sprinted through the toxic fumes and dived to a position next to Jim who was about to lay down fire. The rancher stopped his partner, motioning with his hand to wait. There were the sounds of boots and of metal clinking. Rand counted the seconds in his mind, timing the distance the intruders should have made. He heard bodies scraping against the granite. He knew that grenades would come under cover of heavy fire. Typical brush-back tactics.

The rancher grasped the claymore trigger and hoped it wasn't a dud. He heard what sounded like counting, the scratchy sound of grenade pins being pulled, then at least four automatic weapons burst into life.

Rand pinched the trigger together and instantly the claymore uttered a quick "Brang," then the sound of sand against a wall. The blast pushed the smoke belching out of the niche. The rancher picked up the AK, vaulted over the rim above the passageway, and shuffled down toward the wide space where the claymore had detonated.

The place was a mess. The opposite wall was pocked with blood and chipped out granite. Rand counted six members of the team. The man who had been closest to the detonation point was still alive, his left leg was gone at the thigh, the rest had been cut in half or had lost their heads from the shoulders up. The last live guy reached for his weapon, and Rand fired once, catching him in the skull.

"Five left," he called back to Jim.

He wasn't sure his partner could hear him. His own ears still rang from the noise. Rand crouched and stepped over the bodies to approach the narrowing that led to the lower passage, waiting for the remaining members of the assault party to move in on him.

Nothing.

"Rand," Jim called quietly.

"Yeah?" he answered.

"Two of them took off."

"If you can see 'em, shoot 'em."

"Too late, they're out of range."

Rand backed away from his post, keeping an eye on the opening below. When he was past the bodies in the kill zone, he rushed for the niche.

"That's good news, right?" Jim looked relieved.

"Nope. They'll be back. They either went for help or ammo, or worse." Rand responded.

"Worse?"

"We gotta get back up on top," Rand declared. "Get Amy, and get up there, like, right now." He took a moment and checked the niche, then the passageway. "I'll cover you."

Jim did not understand, but he complied without complaint. While Rand took a position that would cover the entry to the niche, Jim brought Amy out of the little adobe. They ascended the chimney together. Still dazed from the explosions, she said, "I will lift up my eyes to the hills. Whence comest my help? My help comes from the Lord," and she disappeared up the shaft.

Rand knew they were safely on top of the butte when the rope dangled back down to pick up the weapons kit, which had dwindled to a few items. He tied the .50 and the kit bag containing water, food, and ammo to the rope and yanked on it twice to signal it was ready. He had three claymores left, and he knew the intruders would be looking for tripwires, so he put them in the bag as well.

He gave the niche one last once over and realized that Beamer was still in the big adobe. Rand couldn't leave the horse inside and in certain danger. Not that he wasn't in the first place, but the rancher had come to love that horse. He toyed with the idea of putting him down for a few seconds, but the draft horse was the last thing he had that Carol had touched. He couldn't do it, so he led the horse out into the niche and part of the way down the passage until they came to the kill zone of the claymore.

Beamer would not step on the bodies, so Rand dragged bodies and parts out of the way to clear a path, stripping them of anything usable, like grenades. The rancher chuckled to himself that he was such an idiot over the big horse that would probably be shot when he exited the passageway. Beamer getting shot, hell, he thought, here I am totally exposed, trying to save an old horse whose best days were long gone.

The horse's hooves skidded slightly on the blood on the passageway floor giving him the downward momentum to go forward toward the exit. Rand glimpsed one intruder's head that saw the horse coming headlong down the ramp. Beamer was obviously more than the guy was willing to tangle with, so he backed way off and let the draft pass. Rand took the opportunity to race back up the ramp and out of any line of fire.

Out of the corner of his eye, the rancher glimpsed two men, carrying cases, heading for the rock field. They stopped at its edge in line of sight with the niche. "Oh, yeah," Rand said out loud. "These guys just don't give up, do they?"

He stood at the outer edge of the niche and racked off a couple of shots which fell far short, but it made him feel good just to do it. The two took cover, and Rand slung the AK under his arm, went to the chimney, and climbed up.

When the rancher reached the top, he found Jim,
lying prone on the southern rim, watching the two
men below through the field glasses. When Rand
joined him, Jim asked, "What the hell is that?"

"Some version of a TOW missile, I expect."

"How'd you know?"

"It's what I'd use if I had one." Rand answered. He
borrowed the glasses from his partner and watched
the men unpack the equipment. "It's not that easy to
use. Let's see if they know what they're doin'. Never
know what other guys know."

Rand thought about what he's just said and decided
he owed Jim an apology, but he couldn't bring
himself to say it outright. "How'd you know where to
hit that chopper?"

Jim didn't look away from the two men below. "Used
to build 'em till I got retired out. The tail rotor is
usually exposed on the top. Armored below and on
the sides, but the top's vulnerable…. and it was close.
Had to shoot standing up. Recoil knocked me on my
butt, so no chance for a second try. Didn't realize I
actually hit it. Thought you took it out."

"Good job…." Rand grinned. "Thought you mighta
looked it up on the Internet since you did such a great
job on the rocket."

Jim smiled and looked at the rancher. "Well, I sorta
did…. and sorta didn't…" There was a long pause. "I
used to work on missiles, too. I was what they called
a wunderkind. Worked with Kelly Johnson at the

Skunkworks when it was fun. Started as a kid." He paused again. "How 'bout you?"

"Long Range Recon in Nam, recruited by the snoops, did what they call Special Ops before it was called that. Met Carol and quit just before it got weird. Glad I'm not there anymore."

Jim laughed, "This is better?"

Rand shook his head. "Same, but it's a lot harder now. The spirit is willing, but the body isn't.... amazing we've made it this far." He looked toward the edge of the rock field. "Looks like they only got one."

The two men at the edge of the rock field were set. Rand and Jim watched long enough to see one of them shoulder the launch tube, and then they retired from the edge. "Stay away from the shaft. This thing packs a punch." Rand checked the .50 to ensure it was loaded and ready. "As soon as this thing impacts, these guys are gonna celebrate. I think I can get at least one." He prepared to get to the rim. "It's real possible they'll miss, so we gotta stay down till it blows.

"The last three are gonna come in blasting as soon as the fire dies down. When they don't find us, when they see the two on the flats, they'll know where we are, and they will maroon us up here." Rand instructed.

"What about grenades?"

"Not that effective. It's a long way down." Rand thought a second. "I'll have to go down there." He formulated his plan as he talked, keeping in mind the men with the missile. "If I can come down in the passageway, we can surround 'em."

Jim fidgeted. "What's taking them so long?"

"Makin' sure their entry team is ready." The words were barely out of his mouth when the niche exploded, sending a plume of fire up the chimney. Rand took the .50 to the rim. True enough; the missile crew below was jumping up and down, celebrating their success. Rand crept to the edge and snapped off one shot which hit the missile operator in the hip, tearing off his left leg, and flipping him leg back, head forward until he landed on his back.

The helper ran for cover and found it behind a sand dune. Rand waited and counted to seven, the usual number of seconds a target waits to take a look at what just happened. The rancher re-figured his height and watched. The sun was still very low in the east, and it cast long shadows that Rand could see. Since the helper was the only thing moving, his shadow was easy to find, so when he tried to see over the mesquite dune, the rancher had a very good idea where he would be.

Rand decided to go for body mass at this range. He would have to send the lead through the foliage. The helper made his move, and Rand got a shot off. The round hit the helper in the shoulder, and the impact lifted the target off his feet, throwing him all the back to the next dune.

The rancher came to his feet and dashed to gather up his AK and the rope they'd secured above the chimney. Jim came along to let out enough rope above the crevice that opened wider as it descended into the passageway. Rand checked the weapon and slung it under his right arm. "If you see anybody but me leave, kill 'em." Jim nodded, and Rand took one more look below, saw the three remaining team members hurry up the passageway. He let them pass, and then leapt out to begin his rappel down.

It had been years since Rand had rappelled anywhere, let alone into a gun battle. The earlier descent on the north side was little more than climbing down a hill with a rope assist. He could hear the three shouting victory and going through the adobes. They threw grenades into each of the rooms, waited, and then entered spraying automatic fire. Rand bet they were going to be surprised no one was there.

The entry methods, the shortage of personnel, and their inexperience caused them to leave their back door open and to take too much time clearing the adobes. These factors also caused them to expend all the ammo in their magazines. He caught them flatfooted and got two before the third pulled a pistol and fired several shots. Two went wild and glanced off the wall of the niche, the last caught Rand full in the vest and sent him sprawling backward, landing him on his rear end and sending the AK, still slung under his shoulder beneath him and limiting his movement. The assailant advanced on him. Rand knew the look of the pistol and understood why it had knocked him down. It was a .45, and its slug broke one of his ribs notwithstanding his body armor.

The last man advanced on Rand, enjoying his advantage. This guy was not a Latin. Nor were the other two Rand had just killed. His scarf gave him away. It was the typical keffiyeh worn by the Palestinians.

Rand's mind raced, memorizing every detail of the man's face and garb. He was always amazed at how time slowed in these situations. The rancher had nowhere to go.

The man grinned. "Who would have imagined that one man.... one man could do so much damage to such a great cause?" he stopped and appeared to want to sit and chat. "We were on the brink.... on the brink of stopping a powerful nation, rendering it helpless." He almost turned away, but he stopped, fumbled in his pocket for something, and withdrew a pack of Turkish cigarettes. He drew one from the pack with his lips, replaced the pack, and brought out a Zippo lighter. He lit the cigarette and drew a long draft.

"And what does it matter?" Rand thought the guy might be changing his mind, but the old days had left him long convinced that killers are killers. Convictions had nothing to do with their motives. They were just bad bastards; no matter how high-minded they talked. There is evil in the world, and these guys personify it.

Rand had nothing to gain from trying to resist. The guy was too far away to get at, and the rancher thought hard about his next move.

"You see I don't hate your country. I love mine...so one of us has to die. This time it's you." The man lifted the weapon and aimed it at Rand's head. Rand thought "Oh, well..." but he stopped the thought when Amy appeared in her rope seat, descending out of the chimney.

The movement startled the gunman, and he turned his head to see what the disturbance was. Amy opened her mouth to yell, but nothing came out. It was enough of a delay that Rand came to his feet and pulled the assault knife in one fluid move. He crossed the eight feet that separated the two, coming in low. His first move was to slash at the gun hand, and he made contact, knife-edge to the fingers holding the weapon.

He took off three fingers, but the man did not drop the gun. It fired twice into the floor of the niche, but by that time, Rand made an upward move, catching the man's wrist, cutting the sinews. The weapon fell to the floor as the gunman lunged for Rand using his left hand to catch him by the throat.

The man had a grip. Rand brought the knife straight up, plunging the tip into the man's throat. The man let go and fell to his knees, clutching at his own throat. He suddenly brought his hand down and reached inside his vest. He withdrew a grenade and flicked out the pin using his thumb. The lever released, and the man put it inside his vest. Rand had no time. He lifted the man bodily and spun him around toward the outer rim of the niche. The rancher ran with the man in front of him and pushed him off the ledge. The grenade exploded when the body had dropped ten or so feet, shooting bloody fragment back toward Rand.

He was lucky. One fragment hit him in the leg, another in the shoulder. He turned to see if Amy was damaged, but she was not hurt. She stood stock-still, didn't notice when Jim came down the chimney, didn't answer when Rand spoke to her.

The rancher let Jim treat his wounds and sat watching to see if Amy would move. She did not.

Rand made himself find something for the old woman to sit on. The niche smelled of explosive residue, and he wanted to be somewhere else, but there was nowhere else to go, so he lay down on the floor. Jim did the same, and although it was still early in the morning, they slept.

Chapter Twelve

Aftermath is What Happens When It All Adds Up, and Someone Subtracts Something.

The helicopters woke them some three hours later.

Rand and Jim rose and went to the edge of the niche together. The rock field below them swarmed with military looking personnel. The aircraft bore U.S. markings, which did not make the rancher feel any better. He waved down to them and saw a familiar hulking man wave back.

Another helicopter landed near the wash where the SUVs were still parked. A team exited the aircraft and moved cautiously toward the vehicles. Yet two more helos passed over the SUV site, and Rand figured it was an investigation team on its way to the silo. He turned to Jim and said, "Don't volunteer anything. Just answer their questions. Nothing more."

A team made its way up the passageway into the stronghold and immediately took possession of all the weapons. Jim started to object, but Rand stopped him. The team leader called for medics who came up and took possession of the still silent Amy. She was put on a stretcher, taken to a helicopter, and flown away. Other medics saw to Rand's clumsily patched wounds, and then, they were led down to the rock field where they were taken to medi-vac chopper for more treatment.

Rand took the moment to let Jim know what would happen next. "The big guy over there." He motioned toward the hulking man. "He's FBI, and he's in charge here. He'll debrief us…. separately. Tell the absolute truth, but don't answer any question he doesn't ask. If he says to tell him what happened, say you're still wigged out from the whole thing, that you would do better if he asked you questions. He'll buy that from you, but remember, right now, we're suspects. Got it?"

Jim nodded, and Rand continued, "They will tell you what they know, but they won't necessarily be truthful. Parse out what you know to be true."

The hulking man came over to them and identified himself as Jack Peel, Special Agent-in-Charge with the FBI. He shook hands with Rand. "Long time, ol' buddy. Thought you got out of the business."

Rand grinned, "Forced re-instatement."

"Your wife and boy?"

"First out," the rancher said flatly.

"Damn. I'm sorry." Jack motioned the two to follow him to his helicopter. They walked together, and the agent signaled the chopper pilot to fire up. As they crossed under the rotors, the agent shouted "I got a motor home unit on the way, so you guys can get cleaned up, then we'll talk, okay?"

Jim and Rand nodded in unison and boarded the copter. When it lifted off the rock field, Rand got a good look at the entire scene. Men and women in uniform teemed over the rock field, ten by the two crashed helicopters, six that he could see inside the stronghold, ten by the SUVs in the wash, maybe twenty at the missile site, some in haz-mat gear. As they gained altitude, he saw the burned out body of the missile on the high flats, the scorch marks on the ground around the silo, and suited men descending into the sinkhole where the egg lay.

Jim pointed at the evidence crew who worked on the very top of the butte. He took off his headset and leaned toward Rand's ear. "What do you think's gonna happen?"

Rand answered "They're gonna ask a lot of questions. Reed's a pretty good guy, but he's 'by-the-book,' so be careful." The rancher thought for a moment. "I think this is gonna disappear." He considered longer, then he spoke. "If we say we won't talk, it could be okay."

Jim said, "I'm cleared to 'eyes only.' Would that help?"

"Certainly won't hurt." Rand was relieved. "They know me…. might work out." He was distracted when he saw his house, or what was left of it, ahead of the helicopter, making him suddenly aware that there was nothing left here for him.

Everything was gone except the roof that lay against the hillside. The home site was but an outline of charred wood around a dirty tile floor. The stable was a pile of ash. The truck and the Caddy were odd-looking hulks of steel frames and charred ground. To the south, the gray-black strip of highway was unused to the east as far as he could see, and to the west, there was a convoy of blue-black semis rumbling toward them.

The helicopter let down, sending clouds of dust in all directions, and landing softly a few yards away from the fried vehicles. By the time the rotors stopped, two semis, one rigged as a command center and the other as a morgue, crawled into the wide parking area in front of the home site. A motor home followed close behind and parked near where the stable had been, missing the cremated remains of Rand's horses.

He and Jim were led to the motor home where the female driver ushered them inside. She introduced herself as Doctor Penelope Scaff and proceeded to give them a tour of the mini medical facility/clinic. She ordered both men to strip as she took their vital signs, then ran a monitoring device over them from head to toe. Jim was pronounced clean and told to use the shower at the back of the clinic. She packed the clothing in clear plastic bags and set them aside.

Rand, on the other hand made the instrument emit a series of staccato beats that gradually evolved into a high-pitched whistle. He was ordered to stand still while the doctor exited the vehicle, made some noise outside, and re-entered wearing a face shield, a surgical gown, and latex gloves. He was asked to go outside, and when he did, he found a plastic enclosure and pool a few feet away.

Rand knew the drill. He stepped into the 'wading pool' and lifted his arms. The doctor unreeled a hose and sprayer and began to wash him down, using a scrub brush over his entire body. The water in the pool was sucked away as soon as the scrubbing solution came off his body. When she finished scrubbing everything right down to between the toes on his feet, she retrieved the scanner and ran it over his body again. This time there was no whistle, only a few beats, which seemed to be acceptable. She gave him a towel and told him he might want to get the solution off him soon by taking a shower when Jim was finished.

After the two had cleaned up, they were given scrubs, and Jim found a bunk and fell into an exhausted sleep, but Rand was taken aside for treatment. He sat still while the doctor shot him up with local anesthetic and dug around for the shrapnel in his leg and arm. "Your aunt is doing fine. They took her to Tucson to look after her. Dehydrated, that's all. Pretty far into her condition. Nobody expects her to come out of it." She stitched up the openings and set a two butterfly patches on the head wound.

"You'll experience a little discomfort after the juice wears off," Scaff said. "But from the look of your other 'accidents,' you already know that."

Rand slid off the examination chair and found his bunk. He was slept fitfully, waking to hear muffled conversations outside the motorized clinic. Jack and the doctor discussed when the men would be able to interview, and Rand dismissed the thought that the conversation bear a danger to him or to Jim. He returned to his rest.

It was dusk when the two were awakened. They were given hot meals and escorted to the command center semi. Jim was taken inside first, leaving Rand outside with Agent Peel.

Jack had arranged for chairs and a table under a white canopy where both men sat across from each other. As soon as they were alone, the agent produced a bottle of very good vodka, ice, and some sweetened lime juice. "I believe the last time we talked, you were drinking gimlets." He poured two iced pony glasses to four fingers, added the lime juice. He scooted one glass to Rand and raised his glass. "Everybody comes home." Rand lifted his glass and responded "Everybody." They drank.

After twenty minutes of banter between old warriors, Peel pulled a small computer from his vest and set it on the table. "Not like the old days." He punched a button and the screen came to life. "You ready?"

Rand nodded and began to give a brief history of the last few days. Peel interrupted him after he told off his escape in Mexico and showed him a picture. "This the guy?"

Rand nodded, "I called him Guapo."

The agent whistled low. "Very bad boy. His name's Reza Nidal. Least that's what he goes by now. High up in the Revolutionary Guard. We lost sight of him 'bout a year ago."

"Important?" Rand asked.

"Worse. He's ambitious. Not a nut job. Very smart." Peel recounted. "Big bounty on his head." The agent paused. "By the way, you did get one guy that we know of whose got a decent bounty on him." He scrolled the screen again and pulled up a picture of the man he'd killed in the niche. "Two mill, baby, two mill." He winked. "Enough to rebuild." He returned to the interview, and Rand continued.

The attendant returned with fresh vodka and makings, then he hung up a light and fastened mosquito netting around the canopy. A few minutes later, he returned with plates of food, and the two men talked, noticing offhandedly when Jim left the command center for his bunk in the clinic.

It took four days to de-brief Rand and Jim. Peel left for a day and returned early on the fourth day. The investigative teams combed the area, dug up the buried SUVs, bagged and tagged the bodies, removed the silo and egg with the very equipment that had installed them, and cleaned the area of every trace of the war that had been waged.

Were it not for the burned houses and outbuildings, no one would know anything happened. The government sent teams to install temporary housing and hired contractors to rebuild everything.

Agent Peel joined Rand and Jim late on the fourth day with papers in hand. "Here's what we've got," handing a sheaf to each man. "You guys were attacked by drogeros. You ran and hid. They killed your neighbors, tried to kill you so as to set up a huge shipment into the States." He grinned. "Part of that is true."

Neither Rand nor Jim answered, so Peel continued, "It was a terrible tragedy, but the truth can not come out,"

Jim sat forward. "Why?"

"Couple of reasons. First we don't want the bad guys to know how much we know about who and how. Second, Washington can take the heat on a drug trafficking deal, but there's no way in hell an invasion would do anything but get us into a war we're not prepared to fight." Peel held out a pen. "We need your word that you will keep it secret. You both hold top clearances. We expect you to respect it as a national security issue."

Jim looked at the papers. "What's this?"

"It's a contract stating that for certain, shall we say, consideration by the United States of America, you agree to keep this private…unless asked by the President." Peel was smiling. "I think you'll find the terms adequate."

Jim looked askance at Rand, and the rancher nodded approval. The portly man signed, and Rand signed. Peel handed them both Federal Treasury checks for two million dollars apiece, shook hands with both and left in his helicopter.

<u>Epilogue</u>

It's Never What It Appears To Be. It's Always Something Else.

Jim started to leave for his place, but Rand stopped him. "You can't go back there tonight?"

"Why not?"

"Better you stay here for a while." Rand motioned to his temporary quarters.

Before dark, the helicopters, the crews, the doctor, the semis, the Feds left. An hour later, traffic resumed on the highway.

The two men sat and drank under the quarter moon, not talking much. When midnight approached, Rand stood and said, "Let's go."

"Where?"

"I'm in the mood for a walk. Work off some of this rich food."

When they were a hundred yards from the temp housing, Rand stopped Jim. "Remember where your ATV is hidden?"

"Sure."

"Did you mention it to anyone?" Rand asked.

"Nope, nobody asked."

"Good." Rand grinned. "You didn't believe them did you?"

Jim blinked. "I thought it was okay."

"I worked with Peel a long time ago. Anybody that was worth a damn got out when I did. He didn't." Rand continued. "Did you mention your tunnel?" Jim shook his head.

"But they gave us checks…"

"Have we cashed 'em yet?"

"I see what you mean." Jim mulled it over as they walked. "I do feel kinda exposed without a weapon."

"Now, you're gettin' it. Did you tell them about your bunker?"

"They didn't ask. I didn't say." Jim said smugly.

"Weapons?"

"A bunker full."

Rand turned them north then west to make an approach to the bunker from the high flats. In an hour and a half, they arrived at the camouflaged opening to the cache.

Jim's arsenal contained .45s and a few assault rifles that they checked out and slung over their shoulders. The portly man found another crank-up radio as they changed into hunting camos. "Might be a good idea to listen to the news, eh?" Rand agreed.

Jim's face displayed shock, and he pulled out his earpiece. "Your aunt woke up, and she's talkin' her head off." He replaced the earpiece and repeated what he was hearing. "She called the news people in when she woke up.... heard she was the only survivor of the attack.... and she was pissed about it, so she called for a live press conference...she told everything before anybody could shut her up...she's still talkin'.... strong as ever."

Rand finished his preparation and urged Jim to leave with him.

"Where can we go?"

"South." Rand offered.

"Why?" Jim was puzzled.

"First...unfinished business. Second, we need to be gone till all this comes out."

"Won't they be watchin'?" Jim asked.

"Not yet. They don't want any witnesses. I'd say we got about two hours yet." Rand stated flatly. "We need to stay outta sight for a week or so. That oughta give us the time to find our friend."

So, they left.

A half hour later, they heard two distinct explosions, but neither man looked back. That piece of their lives was over, just like it never happened.

The End

Made in the USA
Las Vegas, NV
30 May 2022